THE TREE WITH PINK LEAVES

an illustrated novella by DC Smith

THE TREE WITH PINK LEAVES

an illustrated novella by DC Smith

with illustrations by Deiniol Owen

edited by Joel Pierson

Whistle Pig Studio LLC

THE TREE WITH PINK LEAVES

Cover Design: DC Smith www.WhistlePigStudio.com
Illustrations: Deiniol Owen www.fulmarillustration.com
Editing: Joe Pierson www.reedsy.com/joel-pierson
Book Design and Typesetting: Enchanted Ink Publishing

ISBN: 978-0-578-87217-9 (Hardcover)

Printed in the United States of America

Chapter 1
The Porch

Aching bones creak and echo throughout the old wooden porch. The sound of popping joints and a heaving grunt fit uncomfortably within the warm air and songs of nature. Like a bear rising from winter's slumber, a large man comes slowly to his feet, away from the chair that rested his body just moments ago. Tired expressions live on the tall, weathered man as he studies the day. A scruffy, long, gray beard that covers almost the entirety of his face blows gently back and forth with the breeze like an ocean of colorless waves. A sun-bleached ball cap covers the remainder of the old man's wrinkled face from the midday heat.

Squinting through the few rays of golden light that journey past the shade of his cap, the man raises his left hand over his head to offer more protection for his weary eyes. His gaze wanders to his wrist, where a rugged, leather-banded watch sits tightly. The scratches and wear on his antique timepiece cover most of the once-intricate designs, however the hour still reads like the day it was made. Nine o'clock.

Inhaling a deep breath and posturing himself tall and confident, the man looks ready for what's next to come. A large khaki traveling bag rests on the man's back. The loose straps flow in the wind with the man's beard as he adjusts the fit on his shoulders. The bag so full, it seems to shake the man's entire weight as he pulls it up tighter with both arms. Seeming content with his travel accessories, the man takes off down the stairs of the old porch.

As he walks away from the porch, he pauses momentarily and turns back to whistle. A shaggy, tan-colored dog perks up from its sunbathing nap. The old dog struggles to stand, evocative of the old man, yet makes his way up to take his turn in the summer breeze. Fur gently blowing back as he hops down the stairs with the ambition of a young pup, the old dog makes his way down to the man. Each stair is a leap for the small dog, causing his tan fur to flop up and down with the momentum of his body. With the last leap to the ground completed, he hurriedly makes his way over to his owner, who is waiting patiently at the bottom of the stairs. The man reaches down to give his friend a pat on the head.

"Come along, Rafa," the man calls out to the fluffy pooch. Rafa wags his tail with all the energy that the old dog can muster and takes off in front of the man. Their journey begins at an opening into a lush forest—a trail bordering the man's property, leading the direction the sun rises. A canopy of brightly colored vines and branches creates the entrance to the trail. Creatures around sing their songs while the sultry breeze plays background music with the rustling leaves and grass. The man stops before venturing further in, to offer a prayer.

As his hands journey together and his head bows, the forest almost seems to pause for a moment as if to listen. The wind ceases, and the songs come to a gentle quiet while the man speaks. He whispers a string of words that, much like those he speaks to, would be long forgotten by most people. An ancient prayer for the ancient deities.

"*Vohalei!*" he exclaims as he finishes the prayer. A word that somewhat borders between forgotten and spoken tongue. It's as old as the nearly forgotten prayer that the man recited, yet still taught in children's classrooms alongside *yes* and *no*. It has no specific definition other than to say "thank you forlistening" after one prays.

The man's voice echoes throughout the trail ahead, and just as suddenly as the noise had stopped, the forest begins to talk again. The man waits for a moment more to enjoy the chirping of the birds and crickets before reaching into his front pocket. From it, he pulls out three hand-carved trinkets, symbols cut from wood that he lays on a small, flat rock at his feet. A bygone way of asking the gods and guardians for protection on one's journey.

Whether or not the prayer and offerings do him any good, the old man looks to care not. To some, these acts would be considered religious, while to others, it may just be superstition. Based on the nonchalant composure of the old man, these tributes are nothing more than a small token of gratitude to his neighbors.

Having finished his rituals, the man prepares to continue. Calling his dog along and inhaling a deep breath, he takes his first step onto the trail, a step almost as if into a separate world entirely. Going from a cozy porch and well-maintained yard to a completely natural trail in a matter of one step is pleasantly jarring. It's like jumping into a cool lake on the hottest day of the year. It sends chills down your entire body, sure, but it's the kind of chills that widen your eyes and make you smile without even realizing it.

Reaching out to brush his fingertips along the low-hanging leaves as he walks, the old man moves onward with an interesting blend of emotion across his face. Barely squinted eyes and brows raise softly in thought. The corners of his mouth curl up to create not a full smile, but instead just an expression of contentment, the type of smile that comes more from the eyes and tops of your cheeks than it does your mouth. A face that expresses happiness and longing for things that maybe once were and are no more. Nostalgia and sorrow; two feelings that seemingly go hand in hand. While reminiscing can invoke a distinct sense of joy, nostalgia itself can be a truly unique form of suffering if you reside in it long enough.

As the two travelers make their way through the forest, the little dog, Rafa, takes an occasional lead down the wooded trail. Although he runs ahead, he never wanders too far from his friend, frequently looking back to make sure he's still being followed and wagging his small tail each time his hopes are confirmed.The trail looks as if it was once well maintained. Tall, thick trees continue to create a canopy from the brightness above, letting only thin strings of the sunlight pass through.

Brightly colored moss rests atop rocks scattered throughout the dirt, while weeds and tall grass fill the sides of the path. A bounty of flowers and unique flora pokes through the weeds and grass, while dark-green vines and tree branches cover most of the overhead. As the two continue forward, Rafa's attention is captured by a small creature scurrying by. Wasting no time, Rafa hurries off after the little creature, barking and pouncing as he continues his chase. The old man laughs to himself as he watches his old dog play like no time has passed at all.

Inspired by his friend, the old man joins the chase and jogs alongside his dog after the tiny, furry, crablike animal. The hunt is on, and the duo aren't letting up. Doing its best to evade its pursuers, the little creature pulls off a handful of advanced escape techniques learned over a lifetime of similar experiences. Over a rock and through a log; around a tree twice and then back the other direction. Not slowing down, it rolls through the grass and turns back again. Advanced as they may be, the evasion strategies have no effect. The hunters are closing in, and the creature may be out of luck. However, it appears it may have one last maneuver up its sleeve, and this is no time to hold back. Without a moment's hesitation, the creature comes to a sliding stop, creating the largest dust storm it can manage. Dust and dirt fly everywhere. This is the chance it needed. Having stunned the two hunters with its incredible dust-storm technique, the little creature takes a sharp right turn off into the grass, away from the dangerous hunters and safely on its way until the next chase the small being will inevitably face one day.

A gentle river rumbles nearby, as if to call the inhabitants of the forest over. All kinds of beings share a seat at this wilderness bar. Prey and predator side by side, exchanging cautious glances to one another as life of all varieties comes together for a refreshing drink. The water moves gently downstream, yet powerful enough to create the enticing sound of flowing liquid. Small drops splash against the taller rocks that stick

above, while the smooth rocks below continue to be slowly eroded away, just as they have for countless years. Sunlight shimmers off the shallow waters like hundreds of tiny stars floating just beneath the surface. Small groups of fish swim upstream together, scattering away as larger species force their way through. The frogs rest atop branches and patches of land that stick above. They wait patiently for lunch to fly by as they croak and ribbit among themselves, each one growing ever louder like a group of children all trying to talk over one another. The air smells fresh with that enticing scent of natural, cool water. It's the type of smell that feels like a roundhouse kick of memories and serenity to all the senses.

Having finished their one-sided game of tag, the man and his dog find their way back to the trail. Walking alongside the shallow river, the two are completely immersed in the surrounding nature. Being so caught up in the landscape, the man almost trips as he comes to the first variation in the trail—a small stone bridge leading over the now knee-deep stream. Catching himself on the side of the bridge, he pulls his old body back to a standing position. The man readjusts his heavy bag and takes in a long breath of relief. He reaches down to rub his hip and then up again to squeeze the back of his neck. He chuckles at the realization of his age, as if to say to himself, "Don't forget that your bones aren't as tough as they once were!"

Taking a more careful step this time, the man walks onto the bridge and over the loose stone that almost got the better of him. The ancient mossy rocks have no trouble supporting the duo as they cross to the other side. The man runs his weary hands over the waist-high wall that caught him as he passes to the middle. As he continues across the small bridge, the man takes a minute to break and looks out over the stream from his new perspective. He rests his hands against the wall and tilts his head upward to the sky. The sun pours down into his soft eyes, yet the man now seems more adjusted to the glow of the outdoors and looks on for a bit longer. Slowly moving his right hand around the wall, he begins to trace a set of initials carved into the top of the stone. His fingertips glide over the chipped rock smoothly, like oil on marble. The precise movements indicate he knows the placement of each letter by heart. His dog, patiently waiting at the other side of the bridge, chooses to take a sip of the fresh water rushing by him. The man is so invested in his memories, a sudden splash from his left almost goes unnoticed. Where the little dog stood just seconds ago is now just an empty riverside.

Running as fast as his feeble body will take him, the man begins a much more serious chase than his previous. The little dog, barely able to hold himself above water, and the old man too weak to catch up, is making the outcome of this situation look grim. The trees seem to fly by at the speed of a diving bird, and every running step sends crackles through the old man's body from heel to head. Turns and curves, hills and slopes, the terrain is getting difficult, and the water is getting faster. A few whimpers between the gasps for air are all Rafa can manage as the rushing water throws his small body farther and farther downstream. The man watches his dog get dragged completely under and knows that the moment to act is now if he has any hope of saving his helpless pet. Throwing his heavy travel bag off his back, the man jumps into the water.

The splash of the ice-cold liquid shocks the man stiff as he dives in. His body involuntarily gasping for any air it can take causes the man to swallow a mouthful of water as he reaches under to pull up the dog. The shallow stream has become a deep river and shows no mercy for the two travelers within it. Even if he could get a solid footing on the rocks below, the water is up to his neck and pushing harder than a weakened old body can hope to resist against. He clutches to his furry companion and does his best to hold the trembling dog above water as they're pushed farther along. The old man gives his best attempt to comfort the dog. A tight hug and a "good boy" are all the man can offer. As a last-ditch effort to save Rafa from drowning, the man musters together any remaining strength he has and throws his cold, scared friend to the riverbank.

Rafa hits the bank hard and takes a roll through the dirt and grass. He attempts to stand, but the impact of the throw has damaged his already weak body. The roll pushed all of the dog's weight onto his left upper paw. Much like the old man, Rafa pulls together his last bit of strength to stand and makes his way up on three uninjured legs. Having found a bit of balance, the little dog limps onward after his ever-vanishing friend. The old man disappears completely down the river, and Rafa is left alone. He's given nothing more to do and falls onto his side. Shivering, he closes his gentle brown eyes and curls up in a small patch of sun to dry off, waiting patiently to be saved.

Although the man accomplished his goal of getting Rafa back to shore, he still hasn't fixed the issue that he's now faced with: getting himself back out. The cold water will eventually take a toll on his body. His eyes start to close as his limbs and joints tighten up. His muscles are visually cramping through his wet clothes, and if he doesn't find a solution fast, full-body paralysis will surely cause the man to drown. Looking desperately for his miracle, the man locks his vision toward a large tree coming up in the distance. Previously against the riverbank, this massive, thick tree is now in the process of falling directly into the water. This falling tree may be the only hope the old man has of stopping his body from going under the current. With no other options, the man lets the rushing water force his body down the river and full speed into the side of the now-fallen tree.

The impact is hard and sends a jagged branch into the man's ribcage and calf. Water in front of him begins to show red, and his body suddenly becomes limp again. The man's eyes flutter open and shut; his mouth gasps for shallow breaths as he gently convulses back and forth. When his eyes manage to stay open, the man glances around at his body. He looks at fallen wood, stabbing into his skin, but continues to only take small breaths of air and lose blood with no way to stop it. When a human is thrown into a life-or-death situation, the body will take certain actions to better guarantee its survival. Pain receptors can be momentarily shut off. Tunnel vision, loss of hearing, the body can even convince itself that it feels perfectly warm in a below-freezing environment. All of these side effects are to ensure the body has the best possible chance of pushing past a life-threatening situation. While these symptoms may help someone escape a fight or carry their injured body to nearby help, being pinned against a fallen tree and gradually sinking underwater doesn't offer many solutions that the mind can fix. Without a doubt, as soon as his head drifts under the flow of water, the old man won't be able to pull himself back up again. He will drown.

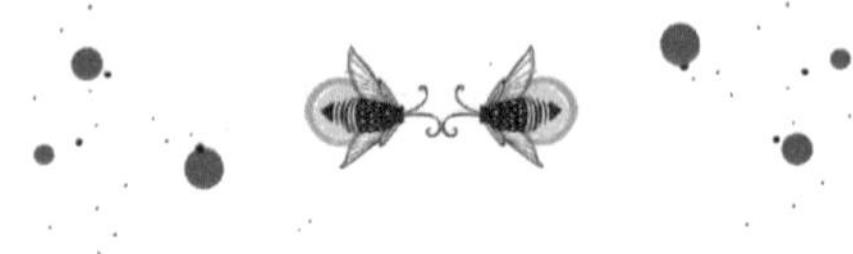

Eyes still shut, the man starts coughing. His cough transitions into a wincing laugh, and his hand reaches instinctively to his cheek. His hand makes contact with a furry, small animal licking away at his face and beard. The old man lies in a bed of dirt and grass, no longer being pulled under into a cold, dark watery grave. His travel bag rests beside him, the shaggy animal now giving a playful bark as the man struggles to pry his eyelids apart. Light shines down onto the old man and his surroundings, but no longer from the sun. Moonlight shimmers across the running water, and bright, turquoise fireflies dance around the air. Having finally opened his eyes completely, the man turns his head to the side and is met face to face with a tail-wagging Rafa. A purple string of leaves is tied around the dog's front paw. They wrap tightly to the canine's fur, and Rafa walks around as if nothing has changed since this morning.

Sitting up as gracefully as an old, injured man can, he grunts and wheezes as he rises from the uncomfortable napping place. Finally sitting, he attempts to come to his feet, only to fall back entirely when he sees what waits in front of him. An enormous creature sits across from him on its knees, just a few feet away. Coming to a stand after catching notice of the old man's waking and commotion, its size becomes even more apparent. The creature stands on the legs of a goat, easily over 275 centimeters[1] tall from hoof to shoulder. A human male torso that's covered in scars with arms that look as if they could bend steel. A body painted in battle wounds, you would assume this creature was a predator, yet it made no hostile movements toward the old man and his dog. On top of the large, muscular

1: 9ft 2in

body sits the head of a deer. Upon the creature's face rest four diamond-shaped eyes that glow the same turquoise as the fireflies, as well as a couple more scars to match the lower half. Fur and skin are missing around some spots on its head and reveal patches of a pale-white skull. No blood or meat covers the exposed bone.

The man cautiously studies the creature up and down until his eyes come to the set of antlers atop the head of his new company. A magnificently large rack that extends out three times the size of any local deer. Trying to count all the points, fourteen … nineteen … twenty-three … until his eyes make contact with something familiar. Being night, it's hard to see clearly, especially for an old man, but the fireflies' glow lights up the surrounding area nicely. Hanging from the antlers are the three hand-carved trinkets that the man had made as gifts for the forest and its gods. He opens his bearded mouth as if to say something, but before any words escape his lips, the creature starts to walk away. It pauses momentarily, as if to ask, "Are you coming?" before continuing onward. Rafa runs ahead to catch up as the old man comes to his feet and collects his belongings. The fireflies around them light the way and create a tunnel of light behind the mysterious creature.

As the man follows Rafa and their new mystical tour guide, a very strange phenomenon goes on around them. Flowers and plants bloom in the light of the creature, only to close back up once it has passed by. The tree branches slither away like snakes to create a path for the three as they walk, and all the animals around go quiet as the group moves by. The forest acts as if it listens to the perplexing being and moves aside for it like subjects would for a monarch walking through town.

After a few minutes of silent walking, the two have followed the creature all the way to the edge of the forest. A clearing opens in the trees to present a cliffside facing off toward a small town below. In the distance, the glow of Arboros City can be seen shining back at them. The old man turns to the side to bow his head and in doing so, for the first time since waking up, furrows his brow in confusion and slowly moves a hand to his ribcage. Under his shirt is a similar set of purple leaves to the ones that Rafa wore, plastered tightly against his skin. He reaches down to remove them and examine the damage, but shockingly finds no wound. Where was once a brutally shattered set of ribs and a completely impaled calf is now just a few scars. The man looks back up to an empty forest. Their guardian is nowhere to be found. The fireflies begin to move over the cliffside, and the old man reaches down to lift his furry companion. As he does so, he notices a rumble in the ground. Rafa tilts his head to the side in confusion.

Similar to how the branches before moved out of the way during the walk to the cliff, tree roots suddenly begin pouring out from under their feet. Falling off the side of the steep cliff, they quickly come together to form what appears to be a staircase, each root interlocking with one another and growing exponentially by the second to reach all the way to the bottom. The man and his dog peer over the cliffside and watch as the roots build a pathway off the cliff, down to solid ground.

On the dirt in front of the old man's feet lies a small wooden trinket much like the ones he carved. Reaching down, the man picks up the trinket and proceeds to tie it around his neck. A big grin washes over his face. To be befriended by such a magical creature must feel like a great honor. The old man bows his head and brings his hands together, just like at the entrance to the forest. Before continuing onward, he speaks a final prayer to whatever it was that saved him and his dog back at the river. He thanks the forest for releasing them safely and opens his tired eyes to the rest of his journey.

"Vohalei."

Chapter 2

The Outskirts

The early rising sun burns a familiar, warm glow onto the faces of the man and his dog. Having made their exit from the forest, the two continue their walk through a rolling grassy field below the hundred-meter-tall cliffside[2] that, just moments ago, they stood atop. The lush, tall grass brushes past the man's waistline as he walks through and occasionally engulfs the little Rafa like a sudden wave on the beach. The colors of distant fields shine vibrantly in the morning sun. Fields of green, crimson red, and even a silvery white that reflects the new sunlight like a sky full of clouds. The old man gazes on to the colorful crops ahead of him.

The green is undoubtedly jhala grass, a thick, knee-high variety of common field grass, the distinct smell being what most likely tips people off. It lets off a watery aroma hinted

2: 328ft

with notes of warm cooking spice that are reminiscent of cold months and snow. Many people started using the grass to flavor their soups or stews about four hundred years ago, and over time it has become quite common in the kitchen. The silvery plant is a supposedly genetically engineered substance called shimmer. Petals on the plant are as smooth as silk and reflect light, almost like still water. The plant serves no purpose other than decoration, and due to its long lifespan after being cut and its enchanting aesthetic, there is a high demand for it in the floristry field. Interestingly enough, shimmer can cause quite the rough headache if consumed raw. If brewed into a drink or cooked into stew, however, the plant releases a potent chemical strong enough to induce full-body paralysis in only a matter of minutes after ingestion. There are few rare cases of people being immune to shimmer's paralyzing effects. Although there are specific races, like the forest-dwelling tribe of Walluts, who are rumored to have developed an immunity to poisons and toxins, some humans have also told stories of accidentally consuming shimmer yet experiencing no effects while their family or friends were left paralyzed for hours. No exact reason is known why some people are affected and others are not; most people just consider it the luck of the draw.

Legend has it that the shiny plant was spliced together by an alchemist as a gift for the woman he longed for. The story is usually told in one of two ways, depending on who the storyteller is. One variation is that a beautiful woman had tasked the alchemist in finding a flower as breathtaking as she. Only when the alchemist could present such an incredible flower would she then marry him. After searching the world and not being able to find a flower that could match her beauty, he created one himself. One that was as reflective as a mirror, so that whenever she looked into the petals, she saw herself in return. The second version of the story, though, is unfortunately less heartwarming and is more often used as a metaphorical lesson by parents to scare young women away from dating. The tale goes that a crazed alchemist grew tired of pursuing women with traditional tactics and decided to opt for a much more sinister method. He created a flower that would capture the full attention of a woman so that while she is distracted by her reflection, he could then poison her drink with one of the flower's petals. Once paralyzed, the alchemist would then abduct the woman and carry her off, back to his frightening castle until the end of her days. Both stories are no more than bedside tales for kids, although a surprising number of people do like to believe the legends they tell their children.

The crimson-red bloom is an unfamiliar sight. Even from where the old man stands on a distant hillside, the plant is clearly visible. It produces a captivating glow and draws your attention into a tunnel vision–like state as you stare. As the old man walks farther, his eyes appear empty. Glazed over, his posture slumps, and his feet drag across the ground below. In the past minute of walking, the old man hasn't blinked once. It isn't until he stomps carelessly into a small stream that his attention breaks from the crimson glow and the man glances at his surroundings again. The cold water soaking through his boot must have been enough of a wake-up call. He looks down at the water and then to his side, where a short wooden bridge has been constructed over the shallow stream. Unfortunately for the man, the bridge happens to be about ten steps to his left.

Luck may just be on the man's side after all, though. Directly across the bridge rests the town of Outskirts. It seemed so distant just moments ago, but now the man and Rafa are within a few steps of the entrance. It must be true that time flies by when lost in thought. The man shakes himself out of his daydreaming state and backs out of the flowing water he stands in. Taking a momentary pause to shake off his dripping foot, as if that will actually help it dry quicker, the man then looks to the town to see Rafa already on to his next victim, a fat, brown cat struggling to pull itself to the safety of a nearby windowsill as Rafa yips and howls after the overweight feline. The man laughs to himself at the sight of such a heavyset cat. Considering its size, along with the dark-brown color, the chubby kitty almost resembled a large loaf of freshly baked bread sitting on its windowsill. Surely enough, windowsill pastries such as that have probably played a heavy hand in adding all the extra pounds to the plump tabby's ever-growing and ever-swaying stomach. A stomach so large that it almost dragged along the dirt as the not-so-little animal walked. It's quite a miracle that the cat can even jump, nonetheless still climb to a windowsill. And although it may not have been the most graceful climb, the bread cat did however reach its goal and escape the terror known as a playful Rafa.

Having removed himself from the water and crossing over using the proper method, the old man strolls into the town center. He calls along Rafa to relinquish his prey from danger, and the two make their way on a mossy, cracked cobblestone path between the buildings. The man's eyes wander and examine his surroundings with each step. Buildings made from thick log and dark, black brick surround him while clouds of smoke come pouring out of the attached chimneys. There's an eerie silence to the air, considering the town appears to be quite active. Lamps are left burning, doors wide open, and even an unfinished meal or two seem to be left out at the tables with empty chairs around them. The town looks like a preserved moment in time, as if every single person who lived here just vanished at once during the middle of their day. It's only when a shrieking cry of pain breaks the silence that life becomes noticeable again. Where there was once no one, now stand dozens of people reaching almost to a hundred. A packed town. Couples are eating their meals, workers cleaning the streets; an entire group of young men and women even stand together drinking and dancing around the fountain in the center of town. The man rubs his eyes. A confused expression covers his face. The noise of talking and music are almost deafening compared to the previous silence that filled the air just moments ago.

The man leans backward, arching his back and placing his hands on his hips. A few loud crackles jolt up his spine as he inhales deeply. After a strong exhale, his eyes make their way to an old wooden sign just past the town fountain. "Celia's Inn" it reads. Perking up and with a smile creeping across his face, the old man and his dog make their way in that direction.

"Room four, please," he says to the counter worker, his words dry and heavy.

"Sorry, hon, that one's occupied for this evening," she replies. Opposite to the man, her words pour from her mouth much like honey from a glass jar. Smooth and rich, her voice rings out like an instrument. "I can offer you number six, though." Her youthful exterior contradicts the way she holds her body. Leaning back against the wall behind her and with arms crossed ever so gently around her stomach. A kind presence surrounds the way she speaks and stands. Even the few words that she's spoken hold a weight of experience, like she's been working this job for quite some time.

The man's smile softens in a disappointed yet understanding way as he responds to her. "No, thank you." His words are reminiscent of scraping ice off of glass. Scratchy and gritty, his voice carries a different weight of experience and age. "I stayed here once. Wasn't planning to sleep the night. Just wanted to reminisce."

The young counter worker turns away from him to grab a glass, her long, blonde hair following her movements like a trail of light. She looks back over her shoulder with a mischievous smile that a younger lad may confuse with flirting. "For the road, then. Don't worry about the glass, our little secret," she whispers to the man, followed by a laugh.

The old man reaches out and grabs his parting gift with a smile, nodding in appreciation. He turns back toward the door and gives a friendly wave to the young worker as he walks back outside. Rafa sits waiting for him by a bucket of water that, fortunately, he couldn't be swept away in this time. The man calls his dog along, and the two continue their walk through the town of Outskirts.

Taking a long gulp of his parting gift, the man shifts his gaze upward toward a large circling of vultures just off in the distance. The man races to finish off his drink as he makes his way in the direction of the scavenging birds. Every sip the man takes puts another hop in his step. Each glug widens his eyes and straightens his posture just a bit more than the last. Examining the remaining liquid, the man holds the glass up to

the light. Curiously, he studies the drink, appearing perplexed as he turns the glass side to side. The consistency is thick like a syrup, but thin enough to pour like water. A slight purple hue is the primary color, but when held away from light, the liquid almost seems to glow a fluorescent green. In a town full of young people, it wouldn't be too surprising for them to be inventing and experimenting with unique brews and fermentations he's never heard of. Young folk do love their alcohol. As he finishes off the last sip, he looks up once more to see the birds from earlier, much closer now. Having been lost in thought again, the man almost jumps out of his boots when he again hears a similar bone-chilling cry from before. It doesn't seem any closer than it was last time but feels extraordinarily louder.

Rafa is just as surprised and quickly goes from a happy, playful exterior to standing close to his companion with his tail tucked between his legs. The old man reaches down to lift the dog off the ground and carry him under his arm, hoping to calm his scared friend. The scream sounded shrill and youthful. Because of the increase in volume, much more detail can be made out of the noise than previously. It came from behind the old man, and although it sounded animalistic, this certainly was produced by a person. The man turns his head to see that his carefree drinking and walking have led him almost to the complete other side of Outskirts. He looks back toward the town center, where the people who just moments ago were dancing and laughing are now all completely silent and still. Their eyes are locked on to the man like wolves to a deer, not in fear of what they heard, but intently studying his every move. The tension in the air makes it hard to breathe. Motionless, the young inhabitants of the town stand, eyes wide, completely silent and expressionless. The man backs away, all while keeping his vision on the people watching him from the town. Wasting no time, the man jerks quickly around and runs. Unlike before at the creek, the old man isn't struggling to stay moving. He agilely maneuvers over loose rocks and uneven terrain, holding his dog and carrying the large khaki bag. His feet land with purpose and precision, and his breathing does not stagger or wheeze.

After ten minutes of running, the man's age begins to reawaken. Perhaps it was the sudden change in terrain from cobblestone to grassy hills, or maybe it was the potentially dangerous situation the man narrowly avoided now being over. Either way, the man doesn't have the energy to keep up his pace and looks for a brief resting place on the soft, green grass under a nearby tree. Slowing his run to a jog and his jog to a walk, he makes his way over to the large white oak just up the hill before him. Halfway up the slope, the man takes a much quicker and more dangerous path to the ground by tripping over something below him and heading nose-first toward the dirt. Thankfully, the weight of his pack pulls him to the left as he falls, and the man lands more on his back than he does his face. Rafa unfortunately goes for a bit of a tumble, but the old dog has undoubtedly been through worse and quickly shakes off the grass and dirt.

Although not the most comfortable way to sit down, the man enjoys his destination nonetheless and catches his breath on the ground. Soft yet itchy grass touches the back of his neck as he lays. The breeze picks up to push a warm smell of summer air in his direction. The man looks up to the sky to see a

perfectly clear day with only a single cloud in sight. He squints his eyes in an attempt to block the white cloud from his vision. There's something very satisfying about seeing nothing but an ocean of endless blue when you look up. The man takes this moment to roll off of his travel bag and lie next to Rafa, who has climbed his way closer to the shade from the large tree. Just down the green hill, the culprit of the old man and Rafa's fall lays plainly before them—a small wooden toy resting in the grass. It looks a bit like a wagon but now just resembles broken wood more than anything else. A tree like this would be a great place for a family's picnic. Hopefully, whoever left behind the toy wasn't too upset about it.

The man looks back toward the direction of Outskirts as he attempts to return to his feet and no longer sees the vultures in the sky. They must have found their meal or have been scared off by the screams like the old man and his dog. The man's brow furrows and his lips come to a purse on the side of his mouth to make a "tch" sound indicating his confusion. Pulling his bag onto his once again tired and aching back, the man shifts his direction toward the gates of Arboros. The sun is already at midday and nightfall is quickly approaching. Rafa takes notice of his owner getting up and rises from his rest in the shade as well. Wasting no more time, the two head off down the hillside toward their next goal. Arboros City is just within their reach.

Taking one of those part-run, part-walk, part-falling kind of movements down the side of the hill, the old man and Rafa look on to a relatively flat and easy walk the rest of their way. The northern perimeter of Arboros is mostly sparse, open forest with a few ponds scattered throughout. Being able to see the tall gates just up ahead, Rafa and the man lock down a consistent pace, which should bring them to the entrance in just over an hour. Much like many times before, the man takes this opportunity to study his surroundings as he walks.

Arboros is the country's capital and has been so for about seven hundred years. Before Arboros, the capital was a two-month journey south in a city called Milak. While Milak is still a thriving and advanced society today, back when Arboros was under construction, Milak was growing ever closer to serious drought and famine. Crops hadn't grown in years, livestock would come down sick and die, if they were even born at all, and the residents were growing desperate. Legend has it that a secret society of cannibals began to appear in order to survive. No one is really quite sure how true that is. It wasn't until Arboros was finished with construction nearly fifty years later that people discovered how vast the landscape was up north. Citizens moved away from Milak, and Arboros continued to grow, due to the forgiving nature of its seasons and new advancements in civilization. Energy reserves that could store large quantities of power drawn from renewable heat sources, like fire or the sun, offered a much easier and more luxurious lifestyle.

Milak began to thrive again once trade routes were established and a common currency was agreed upon among citizens. Even so, Arboros was so far along at that point, it made much more sense to select it as the new capital and move the country's library and Hall of Majorities there for permanent stay. While the Hall of Majorities is currently used as temporary lodging and a formal meeting place for city leaders, back when it was first constructed, some leaders lived there permanently. Because of high property demand in Arboros and the general luxury that came with living there, most representatives preferred it over their own cities. Over more time, however, technological advancements from Arboros made their way across other parts of the country. Communities began wanting their elected leaders to stay in their hometowns and do their jobs instead of living on a never-ending vacation in the capital. Most obliged, however there are still a few who enjoy a very extended "vacation" at the Hall of Majorities to this day.

As the old man and Rafa grow ever closer to the gate, it's clear to see more and more of what was so special about Arboros back during its founding. An almost endless variety of plants, herbs, mushrooms, and wildlife surrounds the forests of Arboros. An abundance of people are out harvesting and searching. While you're allowed to buy plots of land within the city walls for a private garden, the forests surrounding the city are free game to anyone and everyone, as long as you pay a harvesting tax and only take what is necessary. Shop owners, hobbyists, and home cooks alike are all out together in search of their ingredients. Rafa stops at the occasional pond for a drink of water while the old man pulls a thick black fruit off an overhanging tree. The fruit may not look appetizing, but its taste is a favorite among many. The pitch-black peel is surprisingly spicy, so some people choose to discard it before eating the sweet, candylike center. Many people also prefer eating it all together to create a unique flavor combination that can't quite be compared to anything. When chopped finely and juiced over ice, along with another few ingredients, it makes an incredible drink that, although it turns your mouth solid black, leaves you feeling energized the rest of your day. A sweet citrus flavor hits you right at the beginning, while the aftertaste leaves a minty butterscotch flavor, plus just enough spice to make your throat tingle.

The man and Rafa enjoy their trail snacks and periodic drink of fresh water as they come to the entrance line for the gates. All that's left to do now is wait patiently. The old man reaches to the side pocket of his pack and pulls out a small envelope stuffed with papers. He searches through them, finding his identification, a couple of addresses within the city, and a receipt of payment from "Jajahmus Floristry." The line moves forward, and the old man steps up to the gate toll, presenting his papers and ready to enter on to the next part of their adventure.

Chapter 3

The Market

From inside the gate walls, Arboros appears otherworldly. Even at the edges of the city, where the less wealthy live, the whole environment just has a unique feeling about it. Buildings made of shining metal and dull wood sit side by side. Some have windows that reach as high as the roofs, while others are completely underground with no possible sunlight to find them. Dark red-brick walls line the alleyways, and varieties of posters and advertisements cover those walls. Walking through them all felt like being in an outdoor library that only offered literature of one page in length and is more than likely trying to sell you something. If you hadn't the slightest clue about where to go in Arboros, you were sure to find some ideas just by browsing the thousands of papers throughout these brick passageways. The posters ranged all the way from new eating establishments to missing-child reports. "Seven years old, brown hair, green eyes, male, last seen four days ago," read the headline of one. "Stress got you bogged down? Let one of our beautiful women or strikingly charming men caress your spirits back UP!" listed the one directly beside the missing poster. It may come off a bit tacky, but that's just how the city worked. Most people here cared just as much about finding their next bedroom partner as they did a missing child. That's one reason some people prefer to visit Arboros as opposed to living there. That and, of course, the high cost of living.

As the man and Rafa continue deeper into the capital, the old man decides it best to reach down and lift his small companion off the ground and away from the danger of being trampled by clueless tourists and busy citizens. Standing at 189 centimeters[3] even without his boots and just over 88 kilograms[4] naked, the old man hasn't to worry much about pushing through a crowd. Surrounding the two travelers was a unique blend of people around every corner. The man made his best effort not to stare, but curiosity gets the better of him occasionally, and his eyes wander across the many faces of Arboros.

He locks eyes briefly with a Vullac man before he smiles and turns in the other direction. Short and thin, the Vullacion is quite a contrast to the old man. Almost completely hairless, with dark-yellow skin, and teeth as long as fingers jumbled inside his mouth, the young lad raises his left hand in a soft wave as if to acknowledge the old man without coming off aggressively with a smile. The Vullac people can appear quite frightening if you have never seen one before. Contrary to their appearance, they are actually very peaceful and polite people,

3: 6ft 2in
4: 194lbs

hence the reason for not brandishing teeth, in an attempt to avoid potentially scaring a naïve tourist. Smiles are a human formality, anyway. Since humans are the majority among people in heavily populated areas like Arboros, other species often adopt such formalities and actions to fit in more easily.

The old man continues walking farther into the city, passing more people of every kind. A faceless Berain woman outside of her sweets shop, a dancing group of male humans attempting to drag business over to their restaurant. Even down the road, the old man could spot a Fallen opening its doors to customers for the evening. Fallen are usually quite rare to see, considering that they are believed to be somewhat immortal. Said to be born from fallen spirits on the way to the afterlife, the Fallen have no recollections of their birth and come from no family. Stories tell that one day they will suddenly appear somewhere isolated and wander aimlessly until they find a home. Large, gray, feathered wings rest on their backs, and they stand on four legs. Each appendage has a six-fingered hand at the end of it. When not flying, they prefer to walk on all four legs, but in a crowded city like Arboros, standing up tall is the best way to maneuver to your destination.

Although, tall may be saying a lot. Even on their hind legs, they only reach just above 90 centimeters[5]. Everything considered, they are very interesting beings. They're said to have clairvoyant abilities and can even predict nearing natural disasters such as floods or tornados. Six large eyes rest in a circle around its otherwise-empty face, and a large toothless mouth sits on their stomachs. Genderless and ageless, these spirits usually find homes among nature, but this one seems to have opened a fortune-telling shop. The Fallen have no appetite and require

5: 3ft

no water to survive. They speak with the voices of multiple people at once, like a choir of speech and have been known to lead lost hikers out of dangerous trails.

As the man walks closer to the town market, he inevitably ends up passing by the Fallen. Not wanting to be rude, he does his best not to stare again. His goal might have been a success this time, were it not for the Fallen flying over directly in front of the man's face and stopping him in his tracks. A bit surprised, the man takes a step backward but is quickly met with a question.

"May I pet him?"

The voices echo out like six people speaking simultaneously. Although reading its expression may be a bit impossible, all six eyes are locked directly on to Rafa, and its hand reaches slightly out in the little dog's direction. The old man smiles and holds his fluffy companion forward toward the flying creature in front of him. Rafa begins wagging his tail and panting, tongue out in anticipation of the attention he's about to receive. Gently, the Fallen reaches its hand out farther and places it onto Rafa's head, shaking his fur around and covering the dog's eyes in the process. The Fallen reaches a second hand out to scratch Rafa's ears as well, and the little dog lets out a playful bark, wagging his tail furiously as if he was trying to fly alongside his newfound friend.

"Thank you," it says as it gives one final scratch and removes its hands from the excited dog. "Please be careful the remainder of your journey." The old man gives a friendly wave to the Fallen as he starts to walk away.

Putting his playful pooch back under his arm and reaching into his pocket, he pulls out the envelope from earlier. Studying the address carefully, he looks up to the crossroads ahead of him.

BLUE
ROOT
FORTUNE
TELLER
CHELSEA'S
TEA HOUSE

The man veers right and crosses a long stone bridge to arrive at a circular formation of buildings. The old man approaches the outdoor counter of a nearby building in the ring of shops. It's a dreary-looking place with no line and smoke pouring out of the tall chimney above. The man's eyes sink, and his gaze shifts to his feet. He breathes in and out like you would before you perform something dangerous or scary. People move around him, but he stays still. Eyes locked on the ground and beginning to form tears, his breathing becomes shaky along with his hand. He squeezes the envelope tightly and looks back up to the building in front of him. "Place ticket here" reads the sign above the counter. The man shakes off his tears and with a final exhale begins walking forward. After arriving at the counter, the man slides his ticket under the window to a shadowy figure cloaked in a gray suit. Face covered by cloth, the person speaks up to say, "Everything should be prepared. Please give me one moment, sir."

The man stands still, and even the excitable Rafa loses energy when the figure comes back with a small package wrapped in light-blue cloth. Without saying a word, the old man gently takes the package from the counter and steps off to the side to remove his khaki traveling pack. Unclipping the large pocket toward the top, he clears out a space for his new cargo. Rafa takes a few sniffs of the sky-blue wrapping and offers a whimper and playful paw in return, as if trying to get the package to say something to him. No response can be offered, however, except a kind hand from the man to his dog. The sun is reaching dusk, and the natural light is fading away from the ever-glowing city. Warm, bright sunlight is fading into the artificial humming and crackling of torches and lighting devices. The man looks off into the remnants of the sun as it drops behind the tallest building like an egg sliding down a well-oiled pan. Shade takes over his eyes as he returns his travel bag to his back and lifts the now-slow dog from the counter space.

Walking forward, back toward his encounter with the fallen, the man's eyes do not wander. Locked straight ahead to his destination and posture tall for the sole reason of getting around this overcrowded city, he veers down the left path this time around. People pass by him like mosquitos near a river. Noise. The city can be so loud. So much is being said, but not a single word can be deciphered. It all just melts together into noise. The man continues his walk forward, accidentally bumping shoulders with the occasional person in line with his path. His eyes don't meet theirs anymore. His feet drag behind him as he walks. Not in the literal way that you would scuff your toes across the ground, but more so in a way that looks as if your body is moving ahead of your soul, and you're just left behind, trying to keep up.

As the man walks and brushes shoulders with those around him, he finally looks up to see another split in the road, this time four alternate paths to choose from. The man stands still for a moment, staring off into the paths ahead. He watches as people go down different ones as if they are so certain of their destination. They walk proudly and confidently toward their path, no signs of second-guessing as they move past him. Studying the signs around him, the man spots the road he opts to take. Walking down the middle-right path, the man begins to breathe again. He had been breathing this whole time, but not the breaths that a person should be taking. They were shallow, forced breaths. Your body is telling you it doesn't want to breathe, and it's your job to fight through that and force the air in and out of your lungs. The man is breathing like normal again now. The air naturally flows in through his nose and pushes his muscles to continue moving. When your body is working against you, it's hard to feel anything but defeat. The man continues to breathe, however, and once again his body has decided to work alongside him. His hands become relaxed, and they unclench from the position he had unknowingly placed them in. The scowl painted across his face reluctantly becomes neutral, and although no smile appears, the pained expression in his eyes fades as well.

Although the sun has almost set and most shop owners are closing for the day, there are still plenty more that choose to keep the nightlife alive. The old man approaches his next destination of the journey that is, unfortunately, not one of those late-night locations. Flowers of all varieties cover the outside of the building. Colors of green, blue, red, and everything in between line the walls and overhang. Small purple flowers shaped like stars cover bright-red vines that drape over the doorframe. Large white flowers with petals the size of your head and covered in colorful splatters sit in pots outside the windows. A *closed* sign hangs over the door, and an expression of discontent begins to crawl across the man's face again. He walks closer to the shop and peers through the window. Not much can be seen in a pitch-black room at night, however. The man walks closer to the door with little Rafa sniffing and biting at every passing vine and flower and sees a brown package sitting at the doorstep. "To the old gray man and his equally graying dog," it reads. A smirk forms on the old man as he sits his companion on the ground and reaches over to the package. Sitting down beside Rafa, he tears the tape back and reaches his hands inside. A small piece of paper sits on top of a glass jar filled with neon-pink and green flower petals. The man gives a small laugh to himself as he examines the jar. The petals glow like magic at night and when shaken, release a powder that sparkles like embers from a campfire. He holds the jar tightly for a moment before bringing it to his lips for a kiss. He smiles and chuckles again as he places the jar inside his bag next to the package from before.

The man then reaches for the small scrap of paper before getting up. Opening it, it reads, "I had a feeling you might get caught up during your trip. I wish I could've given you these myself, but I know time is important. I made sure to pick out her favorites for you. Please be safe the rest of the way, and if you need anything once you return, you'll always have a friend here." Signed, "Jajahmus."

The man sits for a moment before reaching inside his pack for a pen. He signs the package with his name and a short thank-you to his friend before getting up to continue on. The moon has started to shine in the sky already, and the man looks on for a bit longer to watch a few passing birds. Suddenly, his eyes shoot open in a panic as he hurries up and glances around frantically. Scrambling through his belongings, he pulls out yet another slip of paper, this one he had received at the entrance to the town gates—a small paper ticket with an official red stamp on its back. Quickly scooping Rafa off his feet again and hurrying down the road to his left, the man picks up all the pace a tired old man carrying a dog and travel bag can muster and rushes across another large stone bridge. A loud horn can be heard just off in the distance. The old man gathers even more speed as he hears it. People are now flying by him like passing trees out a train window. His feet pound against the

JAJAHMUS
CLOSED

cold stone ground while the straps of his bag bounce up and down against his chest. Sweat forms on the old man's forehead as he rounds another turn and slides to a stop to head back in the opposite direction. The massive, mazelike city is difficult enough for people who live there to navigate. For an unfamiliar, frantic old man, it might as well be impossible. Once again, the horn from before sounds and lets the man know he's heading in the right direction. Over the next bridge, the top of a red-and-white boat comes into view. The man picks up speed one last time as the horn gives a third and final sound off. Coming to an almost collision like stop with the ticket attendant, the man hunches over with one hand resting on his knee and the other holding the now most likely motion-sick Rafa. Huffing and heaving, the man stands back up as best possible and shows the attendant his ticket. A sweat-covered and exhausted smile rests on the man's face while the ticket attendant just looks grateful to have not been plowed over by a man twice his size.

"Just in time," the attendant stutters out. "You'll be in room seven on the upper deck, sir. Welcome aboard."

The old man gives a sigh of relief and steps onto the boat, offering the young attendant a pat on the back as he passes by. Having barely made it by the skin of his teeth, the old man sets his dog back on his own paws, and the two make their way past the dining deck to find their room. The classic-looking riverboat begins to shift in the water, and the passengers are off. Looking back at the glow of Arboros as they take off down the river, the old man breathes a sigh of mixed emotion as the city begins to grow smaller. Relief to have caught their ride in time, but also an expression of sorrow can be felt among his composure.

Similar to when you have something important to do that you may not be so excited about. You might put it off for a while or decide to jump right in. Regardless of what you choose, your objective is not easily achieved, whether it be emotional or physical. Every roadblock you overcome toward completing your task offers mixed feelings of pride in your accomplishment and regret that you grow closer to the end. The old man takes a heavy seat on the deck and rests his head back against the railing. A bed would be so much more comfortable, but moving to that room means being one step closer to the end, even if just in a metaphorical sense. The scruffy dog, Rafa, walks his way over to his exhausted friend. Crawling into his lap and resting his tired, soft head against the man's body, Rafa starts drifting off into sleep. For such an old, lazy dog, he's had quite the long day. The man slides his fingers through his dog's fur as music plays near the front of the boat. Arboros continues to shrink away, and the man's eyes become heavy like his dog's. His head falls slightly forward, and his breathing becomes relaxed. Knowing he shouldn't sleep out on the deck with a perfectly suitable room just ten steps beside him, he gains the strength and courage to continue on. To some, what may seem like the easiest part of the journey so far may be much more than just going to sleep for the old man. Regardless of difficulty, the body needs rest, and the man opens his door. He steps inside to the next chapter in their story and closes the door behind him to his past.

Chapter 4

The Riverboat

A large rumble shakes the boat. Nothing but pitch-black darkness surrounds the area. Lying in perfect stillness, the old man rolls his shoulders backward as he pushes his chest out and arms toward his feet. Fingers and toes curl as he stretches and yawns, slowly beginning to pry his eyelids away from each other. The empty darkness of the room transitions into a blurry blob of colors and shapes. He shuts his eyes again as the warm siren song of continued sleep attempts to drag his body and mind back under the depths of water and crashing waves that is his messy queen-sized bed. The gentle hum of the riverboat permeates the air while golden light from the morning sun pours through cracks in the window blinds and finds a familiar resting place against the old man's face.

A small, squeaky groan appears to the left of the old man as Rafa evades the sleep siren's call and begins to wake as well.

Sprawled out like a starfish on the ocean floor, the little dog yawns as he opens his friendly brown eyes to the room around him and attempts to rise to his feet. Feeling the movement in his bed, the old man barely escapes another hour of peaceful slumber and opens his eyes once again. Slowly and carefully bringing his left hand to the bridge of his nose, he rubs his eyes and face in hopes of finding his vision for the day. The old man yawns again while his hand strokes firmly down the sides of his face to the tip of his beard. Glancing around their room, the two sleepy travelers take a moment to soak in their surroundings.

Dark-brown wood creates the floor with a contrastingly bright-red rug sitting atop it. The rug is circular, shag, and takes up most of the space under and around the bed, most likely in an attempt to break up the color scheme as well as to help sleepy guests step down onto something much more pleasant than a cold wooden floorboard. Beside the bed sit two small tables, one on each side. Painted a now very faded off-white color, the bedside tables hold a multitude of papers, trinkets, pens, and one small lamp for each. A miniature hand-carved wooden model of the boat rests proudly on the shelf across from the foot of the bed, and a worn-out-looking green fabric chair sits by the window of the room.

Rafa is the first of the two to jump from his resting place. Beginning his day by sniffing around their room, he starts off to all the corners in a curious and somewhat rushed walk. Having noticed his friend is most likely in need of a bathroom break, the old man slides his feet from the warm safety of his bed to the tickling red-shag fibers of the rug below him. After properly dressing, the man digs through his large khaki pack for a while until he pulls out a folded, white padded sheet.

Laying it on the ground away from the rug, the man turns to give his dog some privacy and laces up his boots. After a quick bathroom break himself and a stop by the trash can, the man and his dog are ready to leave the quiet, dreary room and take on the day.

Pushing the heavy door open, the man steps out first into the humid, swampy air. Hordes of insects buzz nearby like a physical recreation of tinnitus. Pale-green moss hangs from the trees on the riverbanks. The dark, slowly moving water below looks just as mysterious as it did during the night, and birds of all species battle in singing their songs loudest, hoping to impress a mate. The air is so thick, it feels like you're swimming in it as you move. Although the temperature most likely isn't much hotter than it was in Arboros, the humid environment would make you believe that you're just in one giant steam room.

Rafa follows out after the man and already begins to pant. A shaggy, thick fur coat isn't the optimal attire for the current weather. Within seconds, the little dog finds a spot of shade and flops down to the cool wooden ground. Already covered in sweat himself, the old man laughs at his companion and reaches down to lift him from his shady oasis. Rafa doesn't intend on doing much walking, so it looks like the old man is going to be carrying him again for the time being. Peering to his right, the man sees another passenger leaving their room and in quite the hurry to the front of the boat. Possibly only one thing would get a young lad out of bed so quickly. Following behind him, albeit at a much slower pace, the man and his dog make their way toward the sounds of sizzling grease and the smells of a mushroom stew. Being daytime now, the details of the riverboat are much more obvious and easy to see.

Bright-red trim lines the walls and handrails, while the rest of the boat is painted a creamy, soft white. The occasional natural wood accents being the floorboards as well as a few railings and overhead beams.

As the two get closer to their destination, the smells of food and sounds of music start to grow stronger. People engaging in small chatter can be heard among the noise, as well as the click-clack of shoes moving back and forth. The riverboat is known as the *Red Regal* and has been charting passengers across the swamps east of Arboros since before the city was built. Although this isn't the exact same boat as the original *Red Regal*, that one being put out of commission nearly four hundred years ago, each boat after is almost an exact replica. The few changes, of course, being to update safety features and newer innovations in engineering to keep the boat running smoothly and efficiently.

The old man and his dog round the corner of the walkway and are met with a small crowd of about fourteen people sitting at a few large tables and eating their breakfasts, consisting of stew, spicy rice, grilled mushrooms, eggs, pancakes, and swamp water. Swamp water sounds a bit unappetizing, but all it really is, is a mixture of water, baking spices, fresh herbs, and mushrooms all brewed together on low heat for half a day. It's really more of a soup than a drink, but around these parts, people prefer to serve it over ice for breakfast. Aside from the passengers, there are a handful of crewmembers scurrying about and a performing band consisting of accordion, fiddle, guitar, bass, drums, and trumpet players. The guitarist also has a saxophone beside him, as well as a flute, triangle, steel drum, and tuba,but is currently occupied with strumming away for his guests.

The two freshly woken travelers sit among the other passengers at one of the tables for a well-deserved breakfast. Noticing the two new guests, one of the crewmembers alerts the chef, and they begin cooking. The old man waves his hand to the nearest worker to call over a glass of swamp water and asks for a small bowl for Rafa. The worker walks off slowly, in no hurry to bring the two their beverages, but the old man and his dog are no strangers to patience. While waiting, the old man decides to take off his pack and lean back in his chair. Little Rafa has already found a comfortable place in his owner's lap and is quickly on his way to an early morning nap. The old man smiles at his fluffy friend and scratches his ears and head as the dog begins his snoring.

As quickly as they sat down, the worker from before is back with a plentiful feast for the man and his dog. Although they still haven't received a drink, the man sees no harm in starting his meal. Beginning with the stew, the man lifts the wooden bowl and metal spoon to his face and chows down. The flavor is rich and spicy, but with subtle earthy tones and a warm aftertaste that stays in your mouth after every bite. The man wastes no time on finishing his bowl and hurries over to his rice and eggs.

Rafa begins to be woken back up from his short-lived nap by the smell of food and climbs up to the table for his serving as well. Although not as big as the old man's, the little dog still has an entire bowl of stew and rice to enjoy while his large companion works on his meal. The man lifts his fried egg over the rice and breaks the yolk to mix everything together. These swamp-dwelling locals love their spicy foods, so mixing an egg on top of the rice like this helps cut through some of that heat. The rice is nice and crispy on the outside while still being soft and sticky on the inside. Much like the stew, it has a rich and spicy flavor, but is also much more pepper forward. The taste stings your throat as it goes down, and the creamy egg yolk helps to soothe the satisfying burn as it follows. After his rice and eggs, the man saves what can be assumed to be his favorite for last. Fat, fluffy, sweet pancakes with savory, caramelized onions on top. If you don't feel like royalty when eating these, then the chef must've cooked them wrong. The fluffy, rich pancakes melt like butter in your mouth, and the caramelized onions are the perfect complement. The earthy flavor remains subtly in the onions, but after being cooked in a sweet, creamy secret sauce for close to an hour, they hold a new taste unlike any other. No one knows the exact recipe for these dishes except *Red Regal* head chefs, and food lovers will travel from all over just to get a taste.

After having finished their meals and finally receiving their drinks from the anxious-looking crewman, the old man takes a note from Rafa and gets to work on his nap. On a hot day, in the middle of a swamp, riding on a well-renowned riverboat, there really isn't a whole lot to do other than relax and take in the scenery.

Some of the younger couples have finished their meals and are getting up to dance with each other around the band, while most of the older folk are heading back to their rooms to get away from the noise. A few people remain at the dining tables, sipping their drinks and exchanging stories with one another. The old man can't help but eavesdrop on to a nearby exchange as he and his dog begin to rest their eyes again.

"Can you believe that load of shit?" a short, stocky man yells at his breakfast partners, laughing to himself and slapping the table. "She actually tried to convince *me* that there was an undying child of Vogh still being worshipped deep in the lake of those mountains!"

"Ay there, ya little bastard! Better watch 'at ere blasphemy or tha' fishy lil cunt may jus' banish ye tah seventh hell when ye choke on them ere flapjacks!" the deck worker shouts back at the small man, trying to contain his laughter in the process.

"Let 'em banish me!" the short man calls back as he stands up on his chair and pounds his chest like a warrior running into battle. "Banish me to the seventh hell and I'll carve out an eighth for that old wives' tale!" he yells to his friends as they all begin to clap and cheer for their big-mouthed pal.

"Wait a minute." One of the younger boys in the group speaks up to the overconfident, dwarflike man. "I've never heard of those undying children of Vogh. Is that some sort of god?" He speaks softly and unsure, yet full of curiosity and wonder.

"Eh, just an old myth if you was to ask me, boy," the rowdy man answers as he sits back down and reaches for his glass. "Legend has it that Vogh, the siren goddess of the Southern Seas, was trapped in a small pond after a storm washed her up one night while she slept. Some locals found her and thought she could grant wishes. When she tried to convince them otherwise, they didn't take too kindly to her supposed lies. I'll spare ya the details, but after being tortured for a few days, one of the men had enough and vowed to free the siren goddess. Late at night, he helped move her back to the ocean and freed her away from the villagers."

The young boy sat there with a blank stare on his face. "Okay, but what about the children part? What did the villagers have to do with anything?" he asks back.

"Well," one of the other people at the table, a tall black-haired Reloneric man, says. His eyes are as clear as crystal, and his face holds no other features than a mouth. His hair is tied back, so it is plain to see that his ears are only two holes on the sides of his head. He speaks elegantly and calmly. "The locals figured out what the young man did and threw him from a cliff, into the ocean as punishment. If he loved this siren so much, then she could save him like he did for her, they thought. The young man fell deep into the ocean, and just as he was about to drown was, of course, saved by the siren. Her kiss allowed him to breathe underwater, and he begged her to marry him. Unfortunately for the man, however, the siren goddess cared very little for human men and instead decided to feast on his organs and lay her eggs inside his body."

"Oh, my …" the young lad stammers out as the rest of the passengers laugh at the Reloneric man's cold delivery and the boy's shocked expression. "Well, wait though! How come you said her children or whatever were up in that mountain instead of in the ocean?" the boy asks back.

"I reckon some birds found his corpse and shit the siren's eggs out all over the country!" the short man answers back as all the people laugh again, including the boy this time as the Reloneric man slaps his back and smiles. "You act like you never heard any legends before, kid! Ain't you from Arboros? I figured you'd have heard at least a couple good tales." the short man says, pestering the boy across from him.

In an attempt not to be talked down on by the adults, the boy speaks up quickly. "I-I know some stories!" he shouts, face turning red. "My grandfather used to tell me all sorts of tales from around Arboros."

After looking at one another for a moment, the group of men around him smile and push on further. "Well, go on then! Give us a story!" one of them shouts as the others cheer and encourage the boy to tell a tale of his own.

Happy with the attention he's receiving, the boy gathers a bit more confidence and leans into the table before speaking. "All right then! I don't remember a lot of them very well, but there is one that he told me and my brother all the time back when we would go with him to forage outside the city walls." Settling down a little and grabbing their drinks, the men around the table all focus in on the boy, seemingly excited to hear a new story. Travelers, like these men, treat a good story like currency. The more you know, the more you can trade. Plus, the more interesting you can look to drunk people in foreign bars.

"Okay, so it goes like this. Somewhere north of Arboros, before Arboros was even built or anything, there was a small town of people that lived off farming and trading. Well, all of a sudden one year, these people are hit with a horrible plague that kills off almost everybody. To keep the disease away, the people of the town thought the best idea would be to throw all the dead bodies deep into a cave instead of burying them nearby. Over the year, more and more people died and were thrown into this cave until only six people were left. They were pretty much running out of ideas at this point, you know? So, most of them were just going to leave, go find somewhere new. Not everyone left, though! Two young people stayed behind. A man and a woman. The woman had been pregnant for a long time, and the man didn't think it would be safe for her to travel. He had been studying alchemy and potion-making his entire life and wanted to find a cure for the disease. Each day he felt like he was getting closer and closer and wanted to stay behind to experiment on the corpses. Well, one day the baby is finally born, but the woman comes down with the plague just weeks after. Not knowing what to do, the man dedicates every second of every day to trying to create a cure. His wife is getting worse by the minute, and the man is becoming desperate. On a stormy night, the man gets distracted from his studies by a loud groaning sound coming from the cave of corpses. Curious and delusional from a lack of sleep, he ventures in. Voices began to speak to him as he journeys deeper. Voices telling him that they understand his pain and that he should feel grateful to endure such wonderful suffering. They say that true suffering brings incredible rewards, and although the man has suffered greatly already, he still needs to complete his journey. The voices begin to get louder and more demanding. They tell him that he can be saved from the cruel embrace of death and that this plague could be wiped away in a single instance if he can just do one thing. He must decide between his wife or his newborn child. Bring one to the cave to endure a suffering, torturous death and he will be rewarded greatly for their pain. The man goes back to his house and knows what he must do. He carries the victim of his choice back to the cave to be met with a monstrous ball of flesh and organs where the bodies of his villagers once lay. Constantly moving and crying with the voices of a hundred people, the flesh calls him forward to deliver the sacrifice. It moans out in agony and pleasure as he lays the body in front of it and returns to his house. Throughout the night, the screams can be heard so clearly in his head that they sound as if they're right there beside him."

The crowd of once-rowdy men now sit patiently on the edge of their seats, waiting for the conclusion to the story. All sit with eyes wide and their full attention delivered on the boy. "Well, tell us what happens, kid!" one of the men pipes up after a few moments of silence.

"Yeah, you can't leave a good story unfinished like that," another adds in as they all nod their heads and agree with one another.

"Oh, uh, sorry," the boy stutters out with a soft chuckle, now reverting to his shy and reserved demeanor from before. "I don't really remember the end of it!" The table of men groan and fall back into their seats, rolling their eyes and sighing at the thought of an unfinished story. "I'm pretty sure that the story ends with the man choosing to save his wife and being granted eternal youth or something wild like that. My grandfather always told us that story to warn us from venturing too far off on our own. He'd say that over time, some religion was formed around the big, flesh-god creature, and the town would recruit new members in hopes of growing it stronger. That they'd somehow lure kids and elderly people to the town and sacrifice them so the people could stay young and healthy forever. It was always pretty scary, but I never much believed it, to be honest."

The boy, now smirking at the reaction he was able to get from all the grown men around him, said dismissively, "I asked him once how guards from Arboros never found this town and imprisoned the people, and he just gave me some silly excuse like the creepy god has grown so powerful that he can now grant his followers the magical power of only revealing themselves to people they want to recruit or sacrifice. Apparently, they move from town to town, recruiting everyone that will join them and sacrificing those who won't."

"Ahh, well, it wasn't a half-bad story, boy! You still gots a ways to go before you're wooing romantic partners, though. Maybe lay off the fleshy stuff too if you're trying to impress a cutie!" the short man pipes back up as all the people erupt into laughter again. "All right, shiny eyes, you're up! Give us a classic Reloneric legend!" he shouts toward the man as he raises his glass in a toast.

Before the Reloneric man can speak, someone else cuts in. The anxious-looking crewman from before is now standing directly behind the boy with his hands in his pockets. His eyes are darting around, and he can't quite stand still. The man is lean and approximately 170 centimeters[6] tall. He has subtle tremors that move his head back and forth as if he were cold and shivering. He occasionally opens his mouth as if to speak, only to look back away and say nothing. The table of men looks on at him curiously, waiting for him to say something. "Something we can help ya with, pal?" one of the men eventually says.

The crewman continues standing nervously, murmuring something under his breath. He rocks back and forth, eyes now locked directly on to the young boy. His pupils are very dilated, and his breathing is becoming heavier and more noticeable by the second.

"I asked if you need someth—" the man starts to ask again before being cut off by the crewman.

"*I need you to shut your damn mouth!*" he screams back as he removes a long, sharp blade from his pocket. Within a second's notice and before anyone can even react, the crewman is psychotically yelling at the top of his lungs and jabbing the blade

6: 5ft 7in

deep into the young boy's back. Laughing and screaming, he removes the blade and is preparing to stab again when the Reloneric man is able to intervene and bring the attacker to the ground. The band stops playing and is instead replaced by a loud explosion toward the front of the boat.

"Don't leave anyone alive!" shouts an unknown voice. People are beginning to panic, and some are starting to run. The short man tries to reach the injured boy but is caught off guard by a charging Maestrdyn to his right. Native to the Arboros swamp, the Maestrdyn are more primal than they are civilized. Standing over 240 centimeters[7] tall and weighing well over 180 kilos[8], these monstrous beings exist for the sole purpose of eating and killing. They walk on two humanlike legs and their body is covered in thick scales harder than stone. Four arms rest on their torso that hold webbed hands and razor-sharp claws. Incapable of human speech yet able to understand a few common languages, these giants are often kept around as bodyguards or hitmen.

Rafa and the old man are jolted awake by all the commotion and can only look over just in time to see the short man be torn apart by the beastlike creature towering above him. Another fiery explosion goes off on the boat, and shrapnel of wood and glass sends the reptilian monster flying off of the fresh corpse and onto its side. People are scattering everywhere or attempting to fight for their lives against continuously appearing thugs and their Maestrdyn henchman. The old man quickly pulls himself to his feet and stumbles back toward the railing while holding his cowering dog closely.

7: 8ft
8: 400lbs

Chapter 5

The Crash

Wasting no more time, the old man turns the corner back toward his room and runs. The Maestrdyn's scream can be heard throughout the entire boat. The explosion and shrapnel must've barely left a mark on the beast. This scream isn't out of pain, but bloodlust. Two other Maestrdyn can be heard returning the battle cry from various distances around the soon-to-be floating coffin. The old man didn't intend to be dying here and followed two fleeing women down the walkway toward the front of the boat. With only a moment's notice, the wall to the left of the running girls is burst through by another fiery explosion. One of the women is sent overboard, while the other is pinned down by a fallen support beam. The old man hurries to her side, hoping to free the trapped lady. Before the man can reach her, however, another explosion goes off from directly under the walkway, not only blocking his path but also launching the old man backward off his feet.

The shockwave of the blast sends ripples across the man's body and facial hair, while the heat from the fire feels intense enough to burn straight to the bone. The old man comes down hard on his left side and is forced to let go of his scared dog for a moment to regain his balance and come back to his feet. Swooping little Rafa off the ground again, the man looks back behind him to see the Maestrdyn from before casually strolling through the intense flames in search of its next victim.

Behind the reptilian behemoth is a woman of unrecognizable descent. She stands tall, almost equal to the height of the creature beside her. Her hair is ash gray and tied into knots all the way down her body, stopping just before her waistline. She has skin of a light caramel color and thin, handless arms so long they drag across the ground. She wears nothing but a pair of tattered and frayed pants. Her body is covered in unrecognizable symbols and words carved deep into her skin. It isn't until she turns her head in the man's direction that he can clearly see she has no mouth, and her eyes are covered by a reflective golden blindfold. Just the act of looking at her is enough to make the man dizzy and fall to his knees. Every second more that he looks on, his head continues to become lighter and his vision darker. Throughout all the noise and chaos, she stands so calmly, as if she is oblivious to what is happening around her. Slowly lifting her long arm above her head, she moves it forward toward the man's direction so quickly that it could be mistaken for a whip. At the peak of her reach, and just before a fast recoil, a loud crackling noise is produced, and a burst of fire is sent toward the man's feet, creating another explosion similar to the ones from before. It's plain to see that she is the one causing the eruptions of hellfire around the boat.

The man is able to dive with Rafa in his arms to an unlocked room beside them, just narrowly avoiding being engulfed in flames. In a frantic hurry, the man carries himself and his dog to the back corner of the room and removes his pack. Momentarily placing his dog into his lap, the man pulls open the top pouch of his bag as fast as he can and gives a somewhat ironic sigh of relief, considering the current situation. Removing the still-intact jar of now-pale-colored flowers from before and holding the small blue package to his chest for a moment, the man closes his eyes and squeezes his precious belongings and dog tightly.

After a few moments of gathering his thoughts and courage, the man places the jar of flowers and mysterious blue package back into his bag. His eyes transition from fear and concern to a sharp gaze of determination. His teeth grit tightly as he clenches his fists beside him. Looking around the room he's in, he stands back up and tightly straps his bag once again onto his back. The fire and madness are becoming stronger every second outside of his soon-to-be no-longer-safe "safehouse." The man looks down to his dog, who is curled up tightly in the corner, shivering and whimpering at the closer-growing sounds of destruction.

Following a confident inhale and exhale, the man slaps his hands together and rubs them tightly as he prepares for his plan. The two won't have much longer in this room before the boat goes under or someone surely finds them. Gathering all his available strength, the man pulls the mattress from a bed and balances it upward and to the door. The fire is roaring

right outside of the room, but there appears to be a small gap in between the flames. Pushing as hard as he can, the man digs his feet into the little traction he can get on the wooden floors and slides the mattress out the door and against the railing of the boat. He runs back inside the room and picks up his small dog from the corner. As he re-exits the room for the last time, another blood-curdling scream from the Maestrdyn can be heard just around the corner. Using all his body weight and what little strength the man can offer, he shoves the mattress over the edge of the boat and into the dark, murky waters below.

There haven't been any more explosions since the two were almost cooked alive, but shouting from unknown people is growing louder and closer. Dropping to his stomach, the man leaves his little dog alone on the burning deck as he slides under the rails and finds a footing on the floating mattress below. Having made it safely down, all that's left to do is to call his dog aboard the makeshift life raft.

"Rafa, come-come!" he shouts, while clapping his hands together in an attempt to make the frightened dog jump. The shouting from before is growing closer now, and Rafa isn't able to find the courage to jump. Still shivering out of fear, the little dog lies down on the deck as the man pleads for his friend to make the jump.

Toward the back of the ship, where the cursed women and brutish monster stood before, the man can now see a group of three human men. Two are dressed in crewmen's clothes, but the one in the middle looks much different. He's large and muscular. Although he most likely couldn't handle one of the Maestrdyn in a battle, he would definitely have better odds than most to put up a good fight. Through the noise and focusing on getting Rafa to safety, the old man can't quite hear what the large thug is saying, but it is obvious to anyone with eyes that he was the one barking orders. He wears a torn fabric jacket with the sleeve ripped from his left arm. His skin is covered in tattoos and has what seems like a branding mark on his left shoulder. Three horizontal lines stacked above one another with a fourth, vertical line passing directly through the middle of all of them.

The Undying Sinner. The symbol, now used by a gang of the same name, represents a young boy said to have lived hundreds of years prior. While most of the legend is unsure, what is known is that the boy was thought to be an incarnation of evil itself. Leading to his prosecution for the countless, despicable acts committed against humanity and his fellow man, the boy was captured by a group of religious fanatics. In order to right his wrongs, they believed in equal punishment to his crimes. He was strung up by his ribs and left hanging deep within a forest to inevitably bleed dry. As years past, rumor spread that the young boy had not only survived his fate, but is still hanging deep within in the forest, becoming one with and having his body merge into the tree he resides on. Eternally aging, and directing those who find him to carry out his wicked deeds.

About fifty years ago a band of ruthless criminals began to make waves around cities near Arboros. Being the country's capital, Arboros is always at risk of attack, but most reasonable-minded organizations know they wouldn't get too far into the city before being stopped. They claimed the name of The Undying Sinner and wait out their days, murdering and pillaging in nearby areas until an opportune moment for chaos presents itself. To have executed an attack so close to the city must mean there's something on this boat that they want.

Some people say they're a group of extremists who found and worship the boy and don't like the advancements of the new age. Other people say it's just a group of maniacs that like to steal and murder and that organizing a group is the most efficient way to achieve their goals. Regardless of their founding, even a group of crazy people wouldn't be dumb enough to attack the *Red Regal* without a reason.

Still pleading with the small dog to jump to safety before it's too late, the man notices something else that may be a problem. Their life raft will not stay floating much longer, and dry land is still quite a ways away from the sinking ship. Staying around is no longer an option, and if the man wants himself and Rafa to survive, it's now or never. As a last-ditch effort into luring his scared friend to safety, the man pulls off one of his shoulder straps and reaches inside his bag. The man desperately digs around, throwing out food, a pair of socks and even his map into the water as he pulls the sky-blue cloth from around the package.

The window of opportunity is coming to a close, and the Maestrdyn from before catches a glimpse of the old man and his dog through the still-burning fire. Slowly but surely, it turns its massive body toward little Rafa and begins stomping through the flames to its next target. The man looks over and sees the giant creature coming their way and becomes ever more frantic as he tries to get his dog's attention. Waving the cloth back and forth against the railing, Rafa begins to look up and notice the scent. His nose begins working, and the shaking of his body is gradually coming to a still. The stomping is getting closer, and with every step the Maestrdyn takes, Rafa also takes one step closer to the edge. Almost an arm's reach away now, the beast looks down at the oblivious dog and the terrified man. Stretching his arm to the point of it almost dislocating from his shoulder, the man is able to just barely grab one of Rafa's soft, old legs as the gigantic foot of the creature comes down onto the unsuspecting dog's position. Falling backward and gripping tightly to his dog, the man yanks the little tan canine off of his feet and through the railing. Banging his head against the floor and almost breaking a paw on the way down, it isn't the most graceful of saves, but the dog is saved nonetheless. Whimpering now in his partner's arms, Rafa begins to shake again from the fear and pain of his fall. The old man wraps his dog tightly in the light-blue cloth and holds him close as he kicks their raft away from the boat toward the bank.

Having realized now that it missed its prey, the large monstrosity goes into a primal rage. Tearing the metal bars from the railing and unleashing another ear shattering screech, the savage creature is preparing to jump into the water after its fleeing meals. As it stands on the edge ready to jump, it is only briefly stopped by the thug from before calling out at it.

"*Hey!* Leave 'em! You jump in that water and waste my damn time having to come get you, and I swear I'll chain you back up in that hole I found you in!" the thug shouts with a powerful, commanding tone. His voice is deep and assertive and carries effortlessly through all the sounds of chaos. "I already got the stupid little bastard we went through all this trouble for! Let the old codger and his mutt drown in the swamp for all I care. Less work for us anyways."

The Maestrdyn groans and growls as it eyes the man and his dog floating down the river. The man is breathing heavily, unable to take his eyes off of the burning ship and near disaster they managed to slip through yet again.

"Are you deaf or just trying to piss me off?" the thug shouts at his henchman again. "Get the hell over here, moron!" The angry monster slowly turns away from the two drifting travelers and makes its way back through the scorching wall of fire, returning to its master's side. The old man and his dog move ever so slowly away from the sinking vessel they were just aboard and ever closer to the nearing safety of the riverbank.

Water is soaking too deeply into the mattress, and the weight of Rafa, the old man, and his heavy pack aren't helping the situation of keeping them afloat. The old man removes his bag and sets it directly in the middle of the mattress next to Rafa. Being close to the riverbank and not having many other options, the man drops into the dark swamp water and pushes his dog the rest of the way to shore.

The water is hot and sludgy. It feels like swimming through mud or pudding. At their current location, the man can't feel the ground yet, but after a few minutes of pushing, he gains some traction under his feet. Swamp waters like these are home to all sorts of deadly parasites, dangerous creatures, and roots to get caught on. The man picks up his pace once he can stand again and quickly gets to the riverbank to retrieve his dog and bag. Rafa is acting much more relaxed now and is ready to walk on his own once again. Gently picking up the blue cloth in his mouth, the little dog begins to wag his tail and shake off the experience he just had.

What a unique ability of dogs. To exist purely in the moment must be a beautiful way to live. Not even twenty minutes

ago, the little dog was being dragged through fire like a ragdoll and hunted down by a gang of murderers. At the moment, however, he seems quite content with his cloth and a few head scratches from his friend. Noticing how much his dog enjoys the blue cloth, the man decides to let Rafa keep it. After tying it around his neck like a bandanna, Rafa runs in circles and wags his tail in pure excitement with his new fashion accessory.

While Rafa is preoccupied with his fresh style, the dripping-wet man now glances around at their new environment. Where most people would be in a state of panic right now, the old man simply nods his head and laughs to himself softly as he observes his surroundings. Ever so confidently, he picks up his bag and starts walking off into the swampy woods, his eyes darting back and forth as if he's searching for something in particular. Even little Rafa begins to sniff the ground as they walk along through the mosquito-filled brush.

Occasionally stopping to turn back and look for the distant glow of Arboros, the man will adjust his direction slightly and continue on. His smile and chuckles grow larger the farther they venture in. The sound of chirping bugs becomes louder with every step deeper into nature. The old man looks down to his dog to make sure he is doing all right, to be met with a carefree smile in return. Tail still wagging, the panting dog follows after the man, attempting to lick the slimy water off of his legs from time to time.

Beyond a few more trees, as well as some vines and hanging moss, a strange, unnatural object forms into vision. Clapping his hands in excitement and laughing to himself yet again, the man charges onward toward the large, faded object. The closer the two become, the easier the details can be seen of the unusual structure. A once brightly colored painted sign that now hangs slightly crooked is coming up just ahead of the man and his dog. Large white and pink letters spell out the word "Carnival," with a few splashes of paint around the edges of the sign to resemble fireworks.

A large clearing appears in the swamp before the man and his dog. The man smiles and shakes his head at the unbelievable luck and misfortune he and his dog have experienced so far after leaving home just two days ago. What are the odds that after their boat being hijacked by a group of maniacs, they'd barely escape into the unforgiving Arboros Swamp, only to find a recognizable place for shelter just a short walk into the brush? The carnival was once quite popular but was unfortunately shut down about nine years back due to the uprise of incidents like today's occurring throughout the swamp. People stopped wanting to travel into the dangerous swampland for a few cheap thrills and greasy snacks they could most likely find in Arboros instead.

The old man and Rafa squeeze through the broken gates to the entrance, although the one doing most of the squeezing is the old man. After dragging his gut through the bars once and then back out again after he realizes his equally large pack wouldn't fit through, the old man tosses it over the railings after carefully wrapping his valuable items in some extra padding made of his soaking-wet shirt and jacket. He squeezes his way through the scratchy, rusted bars once again and gathers his belongings and Rafa to head for the first place with a roof and walls.

A small shack is near the entrance of the gates. Wood and paint are peeling off the outside walls, and knee-high grass attempts to block the crooked door. A stench of mold and decaying wood permeates the air as the man enters the dilapidated building. A handful of spiders have made their homes in the corners of the ceiling as well as underneath and around the left-behind furniture.

The time is only an hour or so past noon. Rafa finds a comfy place to relax on a relatively dry pile of rags and fabric while his owner searches around the close-by area for dry wood, dead grass, and old papers. The building doesn't have a fireplace, but with as many holes as there are in the roof, smoke shouldn't be much of an issue. Piles of old brick and large stones litter the outside ground like a construction site, or in this case more like a demolition site. One by one, the man carries them inside to create a small pit.

The old man kneels and strikes a match over the campfire he's made. Like a father watching over his child, the man gently and carefully nurtures the tiny sparks of light into a crackling, passionate fire. Already sweating from the extra heat, the man removes his damp clothes and hangs them nearby to dry while he sits down outside and begins the never-ending job of swatting away hungry insects.

Probably wishing he had brought a change of clothes right about now, the man digs through his large pack to pull out a small wooden box filled with bandages, a needle and stitching thread, various medicinal herbs, and a little ceramic jar filled with a clear, jellylike substance. The smell is powerful enough to make his eyes water, and the feel is cool against his fingers, leaving behind an oily layer, almost impossible to wipe off wherever it comes in contact with skin. Scooping out a large handful, the man rubs the greasy jelly all over his bare skin and face. Although the smell causes his eyes and nose to scrunch up in a mixture of disgust and pain, pretty soon his expression changes to a look of relaxation. The sound of the swamp is so much more peaceful when it isn't being overwhelmed by the constant ringing and buzzing of mosquitoes and gnats.

Assumingly tiring of the heat as well, Rafa exits his resting place in the shack to join the old man outside. Not much to do now except wait for his clothes to dry. The old man leans his head back and begins to watch his dog explore their surroundings. As the two sit outside their impromptu campsite, Rafa's curiosity overtakes him, and he ventures farther away from the man. Sniffing vigorously, with his tail standing up tall, the little dog leads each step with its nose toward the ground. It's unusual for him not to want to lie around on a hot day, but the man indulges his pet's sense of adventure and allows Rafa to explore the nearby area. The carnival grounds are large and expansive, but from his location, he should be able to monitor the dog, as long as he doesn't venture too far.

Having received his friend's unspoken permission, Rafa continues toward the rows of abandoned booths and food vendors, eager to discover more about the odd location the two have found themselves in.

RING TOSS

Chapter 6

The Carnival

Seemingly never-ending rows of collapsing, decaying, and overgrown carnival booths tower above the shin-high dog as he walks deeper into the labyrinth of abandoned fun. Tall, brown grass fills out the rows between booths, and the occasional swamp critter can be heard scurrying about the land now claimed as theirs. Their smell is strong and easy to pick up. Wet, hot weather creates a scent of sulfur and bitterness among the fur-covered animals that even decade-old layers of mildew can't mask.

One paw after another, Rafa trots along the squishy, damp ground, leaving behind a trail of impressions in the muddy path. The wet mixture of water and soil creates stains along the fur of his paws and face. So many interesting sounds fill the air around him. Hundreds of unique insects, each making a distinctive call of its own. Sharp chirping and buzzing sounds, as well as the occasional low-register hum create their dialogue. Birds sing songs of trills and whistles in the sky above. They occasionally let off subtle smells of pastries and fried leftovers reminiscent of the streets of Arboros.

As Rafa continues walking, he makes his way to a split in the path. To the right is more of the same. Rundown carnival booths smelling of mildew, rotten wood, and their new animal residents. Subtle sounds of dripping water echo off of what remains of the awnings. A relaxing, warm breeze nudges creaky doors and loose cloth back and forth, and the tall grass brushes against itself as the air carries in new smells from the left. A rotten, moldy stench barely escapes through the brick walls of a large nearby structure. Showing no hesitation, Rafa takes off toward the possibility of a ten-year-old meal and passes by a final game booth before unknowingly leaving the old man's line of sight.

Back at the makeshift campgrounds, the old man notices his dog strolling into unviewable distances and begins the tolling effort of standing up. His joints crackle and pop like the fire behind him as he heaves and grunts his way to his feet. Only half an hour has passed since he hung his clothes up to dry, so the man follows Rafa's trail in nothing but his underwear, hat, and boots.

As the man walks to the split in paths, he passes by a number of forgotten game booths in varying conditions. Some have withheld the test of time much better than others, although most are no more than a pile of wet wood and old toys at this point. The man browses his vision throughout the aisles, occasionally grinning and shaking his head. Ring toss with thick-neck bottles and extra-small rings. A pop-the-balloon station that most certainly used dull-pointed darts and half-filled balloons. Even an old basketball hoop with an oval-shaped rim and once-overinflated balls was able to survive nature's unforgiving trials.

Carnivals like these are such an enigma. Why would someone travel far from their home to test their luck at obviously rigged games and spend triple the normal price on cheap food in a crowded, noisy venue? Not like it really matters, though. People enjoy it, and it lines the pockets of greedy businessmen. Maybe you might consider that a win for both sides, depending on how you look at things.

Coming up on where Rafa took a sudden turn down the left path, the man quickly figures out what grabbed his dog's attention so suddenly.

"Chloe's Cafe" a directory sign reads. "STROMBOLIS, CANNOLIS, ZEPPOLES, GALORE! FILL UP YOUR BELLIES THEN COME BACK FOR MORE!"

It's amazing how a dog's sense of smell works. No human would even assume there was food left in a building this old, but nonetheless, something must have smelled interesting and close enough to a meal for it to gain Rafa's interest. Before heading further down the path after his dog, something catches the man's eye.

The final booth you would pass before choosing a direction to the left or right. Still standing strong and in much better condition than most other remaining carnival stations. Because it was built primarily from brick instead of wood, it was able to hold out against the weather to near-perfect condition. Aside from the mud, cobwebs, and dust, that is. Glass bottles stacked into pyramids line the back walls, and resting above them, high on a shelf, is a small metal cage.

Considering the glass bottles are still perfectly stacked after all these years would lead one to believe that this isn't a game meant to be won. Small signs sit against the far-right wall with words "tier one," "tier two," and "tier three" painted onto them. Above the cramped-looking metal cage, however, is a long banner with colorful lettering spelling out "GRAND PRIZE!"

A look of frustration and anger builds up into the man's eyes as he studies the booth. His brow furrows and jaw clenches, but his sight is now locked directly onto the cage sitting high above the bottle game. Just as the man is preparing to leave and move onward, his eyes catch a glimpse of one final thing. Lying under the shelf where the cage sits is a long, sharp prodding instrument. The rusty poker shows dark stains of blood along the tip. Even after all these years the cage above is discolored, most likely from the excrement of what was crammed inside.

A sudden burst of uncharacteristic rage bubbles out of the old man as he lifts a stone from the ground and throws it full force toward a stack of bottles. With pin-perfect accuracy, the man nails a direct hit, and the remaining bottles that don't shatter on impact come tumbling over. Breathing heavily and attempting to regain his composure, the man snorts deeply, clearing his throat, and spits directly onto the carnival game as he walks off in the direction of Chloe's Cafe.

As he regains his natural, calm disposition, the old man is suddenly jerked back off his feet by nothing but his instinct alone. Fear and adrenaline fill his veins, and blood rushes to every muscle in his body. Tensing up, he scans the surrounding area for the mysterious cause of this sudden panic. His

CHLOES
CAFE

fists are clenched, ready to fight, while every fiber in his body and soul should be silently begging the man to turn around and walk away.

Just like any creature, the humans have evolved over time to become what they are today. The struggles and pleasures of past humans make up the genetic coding that decides why people are the way they are. The human body requires carbohydrates to operate at maximum efficiency, so people have evolved over many years to crave them when they're hungry. But just as people have gathered much through evolution, just as much has also been lost. Long ago, before humans began colonizing together in large groups, it was much more likely that a human being would become the prey of something much larger or more dangerous than themselves than it would be that they would play the role of the predator.

Humans have many redeeming qualities. The ability to learn, communicate, and improvise, as well as the knowledge and capabilities to create and use tools, are some of humans' strongest weapons in their arsenal. However, the urge to group with their kind, the need for such advanced communication, and the outright dependency on these tools—this was all ingrained into the human species because of an overwhelming flaw: the inability to fight.

Sure, against other humans, people might fare quite well, but humans are not the majority. Humans are designed to be prey, and only through centuries and millennia of evolution were they able to begin cheating away their flaws. As they are now, with armor to protect their soft, vulnerable organs; weapons to replace their small, weak hands; and groups of one another to watch over and protect their kind, humans can be, and oftentimes are, somewhat unstoppable. Although, take all that away, and all you're left with is an easy, albeit tricky, meal for something else that evolved down a much more predatory path.

And though people may deny their flaws and assume themselves the strongest, the body and soul knows its place in the wild. No amount of evolution can change the soul, and the soul remembers most clearly what it once was. Even though the old man is a product of countless years of evolution, his soul still holds on to distant memories of being the prey. That is what allows him to suddenly move back and away from the steel-like appendage now pinned directly into the mud exactly where he was standing.

Long, sharp and easily as thick as his torso, the appendage looks somewhat tentacle-like and squirms away, reminiscent of a worm as it relaxed and pulled from the dirt. The man takes no time to wait for a second attack and begins scrambling from the dirt and running as fast as his old body will carry him toward the cafe. As he continues to run, from behind him can be heard the sounds of a crying man. Weeping and howling in pain, the noises echo throughout the air and feel as if they're calling the old man back for help. His body doesn't listen, though. The instincts within him force his legs to run forward and his eyes to stay locked onto the nearing café and a little dog's butt sticking out of a hole in the decaying door of the building.

The weeping grows louder, and words begin to form out of the sobs. "*Come back!*" They send chills down the man's spine. Each word is shouted in a hauntingly melodic cry. "*I'm choking on them! Can't you see that I'm choking?*" The voice grows louder and angrier with each word. "*They're in my brain! My organs and my eyes! Please come back and take them from me, why won't you help me?*"

Without slowing for a second, the man charges full speed into the door that he watched Rafa squeeze under. Shoulder first, he throws his old frail body into the boarded-up wood and shatters through it like a stone through ice. The man comes plummeting to his side against the hard, unforgiving ground. Wood fragments are lodged into his skin, and his eyes fill with dirt and sawdust. He feels around the ground with his uninjured arm and struggles to find his way to a standing position. Wiping the dust from his eyes, the man is able to get a clearer view of the old building he just broke into. Rafa is whimpering against a pillar to his right, and just beyond him, another exit can be seen. Using his good arm, the man swoops Rafa off the ground and charges to the next door. Knowing full well that he can't break through another solid-wood door in his condition, he opts for stopping just in front and begins to kick at the frame and bottom of the door.

Cracks start appearing with each kick, and the rotten wood begins to give way to the man's force. "*Take them out of me, take them out of me, take them out of me…*" The agonized wailing continues as the pursuer nears the building. With a final kick, the door breaks down enough for the nearly naked man and Rafa to push through. The swamp bugs' hum reverberates throughout the environment again, while scavenger birds caw on nearby tree branches as if they're waiting for a meal soon to come. Searching panickily around him, the man momentarily sits his dog onto the ground to pick up a piece of the wood from the door and a stone about the size of an egg. With no pockets, the man quickly stuffs the rock in his underwear and bites down hard on the damp wood. Old water runs down the sides of his mouth, and his eyes clench tightly shut as he pushes his back flat against the wall. He takes rapid, short breaths through his nose and in one swift movement uses his left hand to grab the wrist of his injured arm. After creating a right angle with his forearm and bicep, he grunts loudly into the wood, lifts his arm up slightly, then pulls down quickly and hard. A sharp popping noise echoes out of the man's shoulder, and tears form at the corners of his eyes.

Wasting no time to rest, the man reaches into his underwear with his somewhat fixed arm and removes the stone from before. The old man grips the stone tightly and carefully peers around the doorframe to see a tall figure slowly entering the front of the building. The man jerks his head back, so as not to be seen, and tries to calm himself with a few deep breaths before ever-so-carefully looking back inside. Light creeps in through the cracks in the walls and holes in the ceiling. Dust light dances in the air beyond the windows and creates ominous rows of bright and dark.

Soft crying fills the large open space of the abandoned café and spills out of the doorframe into the man's ears. Long, black tentacles slither across the ground and into the narrow valleys of sunlight. They move as if they're searching for something. Hunting for something. The connecting body that follows the snakelike appendages is that of a human male. At least that's what it must be trying to imitate. This is absolutely no human. Thin body and over 230 centimeters[9] tall, the monstrosity moves like a malfunctioning machine, stuttering and constantly shaking as if it were possessed by some devil. Its head is tilted

9: 7ft 6in

to the side, resembling a broken neck, and two empty holes filled with slithering tentacles rest on its face where the eye sockets should be. A wide-gaping mouth covers the remainder of its face. The teeth are thick and flat, most likely used to crush and grind food, and it somewhat resembles an eerie smile.

As the demon moves around the old café, its long, thick appendages knock away and break through solid-wood beams like they're nothing more than toothpicks. Every drip of water from the ceiling alerts its attention, and although its body is slow moving, whatever is in reach of the tentacles is grasped or shattered at lightning speed.

The man looks down at Rafa, who is cowering silently behind his legs. He takes a final glance inside the building and massages the shoulder of his right arm. His grip on the stone intensifies, and the old man turns to his side in a pitching position. His arm stretches far back, and his leg lifts into the air. In one quick, fluid motion, the man's arm flies forward and throws the egg-shaped stone as hard as his body will allow to the far side of the building. The stone comes in contact with a window and shatters all over the ground. It pours down to the floor like hundreds of tiny glass raindrops and creates a deafening symphony of musical demolition in the previously silent room.

The man swiftly grabs Rafa off the ground and moves as quickly and quietly as possible around the side of the building and to the front entrance while the creature is distracted. Being cautious to avoid any stray twigs or dry leaves, the man maneuvers his way through the brush and takes off hurriedly back to their campfire. The man's pupils begin constricting as his breathing becomes much heavier and forced. His posture melts away while he runs, and the adrenaline that pushed him

before is now wearing off. Each step morphs from a strong, powerful stride into a pitiful drag, and the man winces as the pain from before finally takes its toll.

The burning light of the building is visible just ahead. Gritting his teeth and puffing out his chest, the old man pushes his body beyond the finish line and back into the familiar safety of a campfire. Each passing minute in these swamps is proving to be more and more perilous for the old man and his dog. The sense of urgency can be read across the man's expression, although nearly naked, exhausted, and covered in splinters is no way to traverse this dangerous terrain.

As the man and Rafa finally reach the building, the old man wastes no time gathering his belongings and barricading themselves inside. Moving whatever furniture he can find to block any openings to the outside, the man tries his best to create a safe house for him and his dog. He quickly gets dressed in his still slightly damp clothes and digs through his bag to find a knife and a small pair of tweezers. Falling to the ground by the safety of their fire, the man works at removing any foreign objects he managed to get lodged into his skin during the escape.

Life-threatening situations alter your perception of reality and create the illusion of time slowing down. An entire hour can pass by in what feels like minutes when consumed by adrenaline. Unfortunately, It is not the perception of time that matters. The sun still sets at the same pace it always has, and darkness crawls inevitably out of the shadows, just as it does every nightfall.

Chapter 7

The Parasite

Dark is inherently no more dangerous than light. In current times, people are just as safe during the day as they are at night. Sleeping in their cozy beds, under their sturdy roofs, surrounded by families, fires, and homes full of other people just like them. It wasn't always like this for humanity, though. For some, it still isn't to this very day. When most creatures sleep, some prefer to awaken only at night. During the bright hours of the day, they may stand no chance at survival. As daytime fades off into the void of soft moonlight and shimmering stars, however, those same helpless creatures are given the opportunity to become hunters. Killers. Assassins created specifically to thrive at a time when everything else is at a disadvantage—the ability to see clearly in low-light situations; a body designed to stay warm when the heat of our fleeting sunlight tucks away after a long day; the skill to move quietly and stealthily throughout an otherwise sleeping world so that its target won't even realize its soon-to-be-grim fate.

The sounds of chaotic weeping still crawl throughout the carnival, growing occasionally louder and then silent as the cursed abomination patrols between the seemingly never-ending labyrinth of game booths and forgotten structures. The old man occasionally breaks from his tedious job of removing sharp wood from his skin to press his wrinkled face against a nearby wall. His long, scruffy beard presses back against his body like a cushion between himself and the rotting wood. The man's eyes drift around within his head, his gaze exploring what little he can see through the outside of their building.

An eerie silence consumes that vast landscape of the swamp. Every bird chirp and creaking branch reverberates almost infinitely, as if it were asking to be found and killed by the revolting demon lurking about. The man pries his face away from the crevice in the wall and returns to cleansing his body of foreign objects. As he sits back by the fire, his eyes begin to glaze over, and his brow softly furrows into deep thought. Debris occasionally snows down from the dilapidated roof onto the tips of the campfire, only to be quickly set ablaze and scorched into ash and smoke. Smoke dances its way back up to where its fuel just fell and leaves dark stains against the drooping ceiling.

The man pulls a final large splinter from his forearm and releases a heavy sigh of relief. His fingers wriggle on his hand like the tentacles of the creature from before. He shakes his arm up and down and bends it in each direction as if running a maintenance test to confirm that everything is still in working order. Certain movements create a grimace across the old man's facial features, such as when he lifts his arm straight above his head. Painful as it may be, the complete range of motion is still mostly available in his wounded appendage, so the man gives a sharp sigh before coming to a standing position and surveying his prisonesque hideout.

Rafa is fast asleep by the fire, having already forgotten what just transpired. His small body rises and falls to the rhythm of his breath as an occasional whimper escapes his muzzle, perhaps because of a dream floating throughout the old pup's head.

"I need your help ..."

The false words of the creature start to become louder again. Although sound is often deceiving in echoey locations like these, reflection or not, that beast is still out there searching for its meal. Sweat forms along the man's forehead. He frantically looks around the room, hoping to find anything of use. Eyes darting back and forth, he begins hyperventilating. He appears to be entering a state of panic until his eyes suddenly stop. Mouth slightly open, he steadies his breath and saunters toward the corner of the room. The man's vision is locked directly onto his pack. He steps forward and kneels slowly to avoid creating noise. It doesn't take much time before he retrieves the oily substance that he had rubbed onto his skin from earlier. A glass container that fits into the grip of his hand.

As the man unscrews the lid, he begins to look above him toward the collapsing roof. The old man grabs a thick handful of the oily paste and reaches it up until his hand is touching the ceiling. Slowly and carefully, he attempts to coat a large portion of the ceiling in a layer of his mysterious cream before he moves on to the corners of the room. He rubs the walls with the pungent jelly, then proceeds to each alternate edge of the room until his jar is completely empty.

The old man steps back to look at his work, and a subtle smirk creeps across his mouth. Quickly checking the wall, the man looks out to see their pursuer making its way through the carnival, toward the back side of their building. The man grabs Rafa and his pack and kicks away the rocks surrounding their campfire. He quietly opens the door. The old man looks to his left to see the slithering beast checking behind a nearby booth. Tiptoe after tiptoe, the man carries his dog out of harm's way and leaves Rafa with his bag behind a tall, distant tree.

"Stay put, buddy," the old man whispers to his dog before offering a gentle kiss on the head and walking back to their building. His returning steps are no longer quiet or soft. Each foot comes stomping down one after the other while he parades himself out in the open. The man stands tall and directly faces the creature. He looks down at his hand and then to his recently injured shoulder before returning his gaze forward. The monster is already walking in his direction, traversing through the misty swamp, crying louder and louder.

The old man closes his eyes and takes a final deep breath. He holds the air into his lungs and tenses all the muscles within his body. He stands perfectly still as the beast approaches ever closer. At this distance, the words it calls out are almost deafening. Slowly and carefully, it drags its writhing body closer and closer until it's no more than a meter[10] distance from the old man. It wails out, *"Please come back! Please come back!"* The gut-wrenching smile is almost sickening to look at.

Still holding in his breath to the best of his ability, the blue-faced man precisely throws his ceramic jar against the door of their building, two meters beside him. At breakneck

10: 3ft

speed, the creature jerks its attention to the noise and sends its arm flying toward the sounds of the breaking jar, straight through the flimsy door. It lets out an ear-piercing shriek as the tentacle-like appendage lands near the campfire. It jolts its arm back quickly and begins moving in the building's direction.

The old man hasn't even blinked. Eyes piercing directly through the wretched hellspawn walking before him. Slowly releasing his breath as the beast walks farther away, the old man's eyes grow wide, and the smirk from before returns to his mouth. He reaches down and grabs a plentiful handful of pebbles and sand. At the exact moment that the creature enters the building, the man releases his shrapnel, catapulting it through the air and directly on top of the weak, decaying roof. The monster's arms go flying everywhere. Like a cyclone of whips, they crack against the ceiling and walls in a flurry of destruction. Just like that, the brick hut comes crashing down right onto the beast and the campfire. The man begins running back toward his dog and bag while the creature wails in pain and a thick black smoke forms in the rubble. The pungent smell of burning ointment is strong; it puts tears in the man's eyes, even at his current distance.

Words no longer escape the creature's mouth; only screams as it burns underneath the destruction. The collapsed building is scorching and cooking the creature like a furnace. Brick and debris are flying everywhere as it tries to escape the fiery trap, but the man and Rafa are already nearing the café, passing through and moving southeast, away from the falling sun.

The screams stop. The swamp grows quiet, if only for a minute. Barely outside and past Chloe's Cafe, the brick wall comes crashing down behind the two fleeing travelers. The man looks back briefly, then immediately continues running forward. As if things couldn't get any worse, just behind the man and his dog lies a Maestrdyn, having just broken through the wall. It struggles to regain its footing and appears to be unfamiliar with its own body. The reptilelike beast writhes on the ground in agony and unleashes a bone-chilling roar. The man can hear its skeleton being shattered and the sounds of flesh tearing apart with each scream of the beast. It wasn't chasing the old man; it was fleeing too. It must have heard the commotion from before and showed up for an easy meal just as the old man and Rafa left the abomination to burn. Although now, It's much clearer exactly what that abomination is. A parasite.

The Maestrdyn claws and tears away at its own flesh. Charging into trees and walls, the beast cries out with every breath it can suffer out. Tentacles begin snaking their way out of the large, bulging eye sockets of the Maestrdyn's head. They weave in and out of the struggling beast like serpents, throbbing and pulsating. Not a single drop of blood has fallen from the creature's body. Each droplet is quickly caught by one of the many black tentacles wrapping around the soon-to-be corpse. Nothing will be left behind to rot. The parasitic monster is quickly and efficiently draining every source of life from the towering Maestrdyn as if it were no challenge at all.

The air smells bitter, with subtle notes of charred flesh. The screams of the enormous creature are being muffled by a colony of tentacles forming inside its throat, cascading out like a pitch-black waterfall. Before long, the Maestrdyn is pinned face down against the dirt, all six limbs stretched out in a cross formation. The tentacles weave in and out of its skin like chains, digging deep into the ground to keep the beast immobile. Its

cries can no longer be heard, just the sounds of bones being ground away into dust.

With each bite that the parasite consumes, the wounds across its body from the impromptu napalm trap and Maestrdyn begin to repair themselves. A slimy coating pours out of its skin and solidifies into new tentacles where the wounds once were. The parasite begins to slow its feeding process. It gradually moves its nightmarish, demonic face toward the single uninjured location that remains on the Maestrdyn's body—the back of its head. The eye tentacles of the parasite shoot forward quickly, like spears directly into the skull of its meal. Each piercing strike sends shocks and convulsions throughout the body of the dying Maestrdyn.

For a moment, everything becomes motionless. The tentacles of the parasite slowly snake their way out of the Maestrdyn's arms and legs, freeing them from the ground. It begins to take a new position across the fresh corpse. Lying flat against its back, the parasite starts to match the position of its body to that of the Maestrdyn, like a shadow that never left the body. Subtle movements and twitches come from the fingers of the fallen beast. Its body convulses and shakes, but sure enough, begins to move again. The webbed hands come to a pushup position as its legs kick around in the dirt. Quickly it launches itself from the ground to a tall standing position. Tentacles still pour out of its eyes and mouth, but it moves around as if nothing is happening.

Looming just behind the Maestrdyn is the silhouette of its killer. Its head and shoulders hover practically a meter above the reanimated body, smiling. Tentacles hang down from its dark black figure, piercing into all locations of the Maestrdyn, moving the body around like strings on a marionette. The back of its head is still connected to the now-much-longer tentacles that flow from the parasite's eye sockets. They pulse as if they're constantly sucking something from the creature's brain—or possibly depositing something instead.

The old man and Rafa continue to run. No longer caring about the sounds of his footsteps, he flees as quickly as his old, tired body is capable. It no longer matters anyway. The parasite controls its meal like a toy. Like it owns the body. It moves quickly now, perhaps even faster than the Maestrdyn was capable of before. Powering toward the sounds of the old man and his dog, the hybrid beast effortlessly plows through trees and branches. What the puppetlike arms of the Maestrdyn can't demolish, one of the many tentacles exploding from its back does.

Fighting is impossible. Running is useless. Pleading won't be an option, and shelter is nowhere to be seen. Dying is the correct option in this circumstance. The world has created four creatures: a small, frail dog; a weak old man; a monstrous killing machine that moves through stone like it was fabric; and the parasitic abomination controlling it from behind.

The old man carries onward, dodging low-hanging branches and trying his best to maneuver over rocks and difficult terrain. Dirt has transitioned into swampy mud. Each step of the man takes longer than the last to pull from the ground. The old man looks down to his dog with sadness in his eyes. He holds Rafa close to his chest and crouches as the beast approaches. Although his dog trembles with fear, the old man just breathes. Eyes closed, arms wrapped around his friend, and teeth gritted tightly in anticipation.

He squeezes his dog tightly, covering Rafa's ears with his old, wrinkled hands. The parasite can be heard weeping again in the distance, however, this time it sounds more like a laugh. As the noises become louder and louder, Rafa squirms and shakes in the old man's grasp. As if he were trying to escape his owner's hold, the dog moves around and kicks his legs back and forth. The old man notices this and opens his eyes to a squint. His vision begins at Rafa but sluggishly moves up to a bright light in front of him, a polychromatic pillar of light, barely escaping through the cracks of a nearby boulder. Each passing second, the light grows stronger and brighter. With nothing to lose, the man gathers what little strength he has and drags his way across the muddy swamp to the glowing stone. The light is almost blinding by the time the man reaches his target. Although not much can be seen through the color-changing beam of radiance, it vaguely appears as if the boulder were opening up; a hole forming at the top, beginning no bigger than a crack, but now just large enough for the man's backpack to be dropped inside.

The parasite-controlled Maestrdyn is within striking distance. With nothing left to lose, the old man drops his dog and bag inside the glaring hole. He glances up to see the pillar of light shining directly into the sun before attempting to drop in next, pushing his body feet-first in the hole after Rafa and his bag. Unfortunately, his shoulders appear to be just too wide to slide through. The beast now stands directly above the trapped old man. He struggles and shakes to fall down but moves not a single inch. The rock is no longer expanding, and the man's feet have yet to touch solid ground where he might gather a footing.

Panic is setting into his face again. The man looks desperately around for anything that may be of help, but from his position, he may as well be served on a silver platter. As the Maestrdyn takes its final step forward, a long, black tentacle rears back. The old man inhales a deep breath and throws his forehead full speed against the side of the rock, as far away as his body will stretch, creating a loud collision sound. He swiftly recoils away from the point of impact just as the parasite flings its whiplike appendage forward. All within a second, and before the blood from the old man's head even leaves his skin, the tentacle jolts directly into the stone. It spears through the rock at the precise location where the man slammed his face and shatters the boulder just enough for him to fall unconscious through the pit.

His body ragdolls down a narrow tunnel of reflective, mirrorlike stone, sliding, twisting, and turning as it travels deeper and deeper into the ground. The hole above closes up rapidly and simultaneously as the pillar of light from before appears to reflect off of the sky and travel back down into the tunnel after the old man. Before long, the light has escaped past the unconscious old man, and he's left falling aimlessly into darkness. His body eventually hits ground. If he were awake to feel it, it wouldn't have been a pleasant landing. Dropping two meters onto more mirrorlike stones, his body lies limp and motionless.

The floor is perfectly smooth, albeit hard, and the walls consist of more of the same silver, reflective rocks. They make up almost the entire cavern. No more than two meters high and one meter wide where the man landed, the claustrophobic, pyramid-shaped room tapers off toward the back but then opens up to a much larger square-shaped hallway. Even with no natural light, the cavern and hallway emanate a gentle polychromatic glow identical to the pillar above. It's as if the light was trapped within the reflective stones, shimmering and radiating a warm, relaxing temperature.

Rafa trots over to his companion, lying unmoving on the ground. His large bag must have rolled once it landed, because nothing was there to break the old man's fall. The walls and floor, along with their glow, also release a melodic drone, as if multiple people at once were all humming the same tune. Rafa licks the old man's face, then retreats to his stomach to lie beside him until he awakens.

Chapter 8

The Depths

A tired groan barely escapes the man's throat. His eyes clench tightly as a grimace forms across his face. Another groan, this time more audible. The man moves around, trying to find his balance. He first rolls to his side, then to all fours. He reaches up to clutch his forehead but jerks away at the feeling of his touch. His eyes struggle to open through the dried blood coated over them. His right hand moves up to wipe them clean, while his left he uses for balance to stand up. Almost immediately hitting his head while standing in the short room, the man falls back on his tailbone and lets out a defeated, tired sigh. Rafa notices the movement and wakes from his nap to check on his old friend.

Having now scrubbed away enough of the dried blood to begin opening his eyes, the old man peers through blurry vision to find his dog. He reaches out a comforting hand and pets his small, furry companion.

"Good boy, Rafa. Thank you for staying with me out there, friend." His words are hoarse but warm. Even through blood-covered eyes, after being chased by the parasitic hunter in a cursed swamp, the love for his pet is painted clearly across the old man's expression. "I wish I had some water for us." He coughs out the dry, scratchy words. The old man clears his throat and looks at their surroundings. "Certainly isn't the most peculiar place we've found ourselves in, eh, old boy?" Rafa barks back and wags his tail. The old man laughs at the bottomless positivity from his four-legged friend.

He begins to stand again, this time being spatially aware, and surveys the room to find his bag. He spots it sitting against a wall and walks over to retrieve his precious belongings. Lifting the bag from the ground, tears well up in the man's eyes. He looks toward the glowing hallway, then back toward his backpack. The old man takes his time placing the bag on his back and fixing the straps, just as he did when he started his journey. He looks down toward Rafa, who is entranced by his reflection in the colorful, glowing stones. He smiles and wipes the tears from his eyes before calling Rafa to his side.

"We'll find a way out of here. Please hold on a bit longer, dear," he whispers to himself, then pats his leg. With a quick two-toned whistle, he captures his dog's attention then motions with his hand for Rafa to follow. The old dog strolls over very slowly, then immediately lies down at the man's feet. Rafa isn't known to be the quickest in the land, but even this is much slower than his usual pace. "You okay, pal?" the old man asks his dog. An expression of sympathy and sadness lurks across his face. These two have been through a lot together. The man breathes in, then smiles warmly at his pup. He reaches down and lifts the weary dog from its feet and holds him tightly to his chest. "Don't worry, Rafa dog, I can always give you a lift," he says with a chuckle.

The old man and Rafa look down the long, winding path ahead of them. There's no going back up, not like any sane person would even want to, with that parasite on the loose. The path curves back and forth and eventually makes a sharp right turn. Beyond that turn, nothing can be seen from the old man's point of view. The only way to discover is to adventure forward.

As the man takes the first step out of the cavern and into the winding tunnel, he pauses for a moment longer to look back. The room is so mysterious. A magical tunnel just happened to open up and release a blinding beam of light for no reason? That wouldn't be the most bizarre occurrence to happen around this world, but still. If one thing is for certain, even unexplainable circumstances have a cause and effect.

The man turns back and begins walking down the hallway. What starts out as a square-shaped tunnel transitions to hexagonal. The light from before still hums off of the glowing walls. It doesn't appear to be naturally made, but what could even create such a curious place?

The underground air is cool and fresh. The old man takes in a deep gulp of air, and his eyes widen at the taste of delicious oxygen his lungs just received. His steps become faster and more confident with every passing stride. Chills bubble across his skin as he journeys deeper. The fur on Rafa's body begins to rise and fall. Before long, even the beard on the old man's face is standing at attention, just like his dog's thick coat. It's as if the two adventurers were sliding around on carpet.

Tiny jolts of multicolored static burst from the rock walls and floor, bouncing off the old man and Rafa. The man jumps back at the sight of one running across his body but relaxes his guard as he studies it closer. Holding Rafa in his right arm, the man lifts his left hand closer to his eyes and carefully inspects the color-changing static. It dances around his body, never being completely still or coming detached from a rock face. He turns his hand over to watch both sides before waving it through a small jolt attached to Rafa's body, as if he were trying to chop through a thread with his bare hand.

His hand glides right through with no resistance. Momentarily, the static connects to him, but as his hand passes, it returns it to his dog. Cautiously he steps forward as more static jolts form off the rocks, overtaking his and Rafa's bodies. What began as one or two is multiplying into the hundreds. Constantly moving, bumping against, and forming with one another, the peculiar static has no physical effects other than leaving a quickly fleeting trail of fluorescent color where it touches. Painting scribbled neon ribbons across the old man and his dog, the static continues to multiply with each step farther into the tunnel.

By the time the two have reached the end of their passageway, the static is almost blinding. It's as if they are completely enveloped in the pillar of light from before. Except this time, the colorful light only glows from themselves and the hallway. No beam reaching to the heavens. It covers every centimeter of their bodies aside from their eyes. The old man and Rafa are completely glowing, the colorful lights swirling around their skin and clothes like a pool of neon liquid. Whenever one of the two breathes, a cloud of icy condensation pours out. It looks reminiscent of being outside on a frigid day in the winter, but the cave and static feel comfortably warm.

The hexagonal hallway of lights and static comes to a sudden stop just ahead of the two adventurers. Within a few more steps, they'll find themselves in a pitch-black abyss with no more colorful lights to guide them. The old man steps out carefully, to avoid falling into some bottomless pit. Unexpectedly, his foot hits something solid at the exact same level of their current floor. Colorful snakelike strands slither away from his foot the moment it lands. They break off in multiple directions and wriggle away, slowly fading into the darkness around them. As the man and Rafa pass through into the darkness, the static is left behind at the end of the hallway. It stretches to stay attached to the old man and his dog but is quickly snapped away from them as they move through the opening. The colorful lights, however, still coat their bodies and mix around aimlessly, just as they did in the hallway.

Every step creates the same effect as his first, releasing colorful strands of light from his feet to slither away into nothingness. The old man walks forward into the void, slowly becoming more sure of his footing. Looking behind them, the old man notices a subtle trail of light being left in the air as the two move. Just like the colors from his feet, it too fades away as they move farther in.

The old man reaches out his left hand to caress the empty space around him but shockingly is stopped against something solid. Colorful worms pour from his fingertips, similar to his feet, except these appear to have more purpose. Instead of immediately fading away like the ones below and around him, these colors begin to draw crude shapes. Only simple shapes such as squares and circles at first, but then they go about to act differently. They come together across the pitch-black, unseeable wall and create an image of wings. The wings float around for a moment, flapping upward, then swooping back down before exploding into a shimmering display and sizzling away into darkness.

Entranced by the image, the man returns his hand to the unseeable wall, this time with more force. He rubs his palm quickly across the wall, unleashing a horde of colorful worms to dance about. Some fade away after becoming rudimentary outlines again, while others come together into a grand exhibit of light and motion. Trees swaying in a breeze as their falling leaves morph into a variety of birds and fish. The birds fly upward, while the fish swim deep down toward the man's feet.

The old man continues rubbing the wall, quickly and all over. He begins tapping his feet against the ground and walking back and forth to see all the moving images. Rafa stays motionless in the man's arm, equally captivated by the show put on before them. The room becomes brighter with each touch and movement of the old man. Fish swimming below get caught in nets by people on boats, while the people in boats get swallowed up and dragged away by monstrous leviathans. Birds above dive into clouds and melt away into a colorful rain that pours down across the ground. Each drop of the rain builds into a delicate flower or towering mountain. Some into small people that wander about the vibrant, fleeting landscape. They fight among each other and sleep in small houses. Some grow crops, while others can be seen eating at expansive tables with friends and family. Creatures and environments of a never-ending variety are brought to life then swept away in a matter of seconds as the old man and his dog walk around the room. Butterflies begin to form out of the colorful remnants of other creatures and slowly swarm around, consuming the old man and dog. They spin in circles and travel upward like a tornado until hitting what now looks to be a ceiling.

All at once, the butterflies pour to the ground like a crashing wave and engulf the two travelers. The room goes black again. The old man and Rafa have lost all their shining color and now stand motionless in the infinite black void. The man looks to his sides and touches the walls and floor, but nothing comes from his fingertips now. Above the man, a small shining star can be seen, what feels like millions of kilometers[11] away. He squints and attempts to focus on the celestial light. A second comes to life beside it, and from that one another. They multiply off of each other, some large and some small. They form on the floor and the ceiling. The walls and even the empty space around the old man and his dog are filled with tens of thousands of beautiful, shining stars. They change in color and twinkle about like a magnificent night sky. Once again, the room begins to fill with light in every direction. Standing in the middle of it looks and feels like floating throughout space.

The old man walks forward, and as he does, the stars around him pour down at his feet to build a staircase. One by one, the stairs are created underneath the man's feet and lead him directly down. Just moments ago, this room appeared to have a completely flat floor and walls, but now the man and his dog are plainly walking down through the invisible floor on a staircase built from starlight. The stairs weave up and down, through all different directions, before eventually coming to a

11: 1km = 0.6 miles

gigantic stone door. The man walks to its side and peers behind the ten-meter-high[12] door to see nothing but black. He looks back to where he just was and sees more of the same. Returning to the front of the monolithic door, the stars are now circling up its sides and across its front.

The man takes a step back and looks upward as the stars fly and swing about the massive passageway. Suddenly they stop, remaining completely still where they landed. They begin to hum, similar to the walls from before, and pulsate as if they are waiting for something to happen. The old man looks down at his little dog and back to the tall stone door. Stepping forward, he pushes his left hand out, and his fingertips brush against the rock. A loud ringing sound reverberates from the door like someone just hit a giant bell. It rings again as a long crevice appears at the very top of the door. Gradually the crevice widens, revealing a gigantic eye that looks to be alive inside of the stone. The rock on the door moves and morphs. It almost gives the illusion of breathing as the door throbs in and out. Another bell rings, this time much softer, and another crevice forms. Another enormous eye opens up, just like the first, and peers down at the old man and his dog.

One after another, this continues to happen until six large eyes have formed and stare directly at the two creatures standing before them. The colossal door continues to throb in and out while the eyes look to one another's directions and around the empty void. Echoing out like a choir of thousands of people, unfamiliar and indescribable noise is created by the door. It sounds as if it were trying to say something to the two travelers, but its language is completely incomprehensible for the minds of a human and dog.

12: 30ft

Abruptly the snakelike colors from before slither forward, past the old man's feet and toward the door. Still looking up at the humongous eyes, the man and his dog take no notice of the colorful worms forming out of the void and sliding right past them. Beginning at the bottom of the gargantuan door, the colors drag themselves up its side and over the top. As they pass over the stone door, they leave behind a unique set of runes unlike any written in notable texts. The runes arch their way up from the bottom left and right and meet at the very top center above the first eye that was revealed.

With not a single warning, the stone door begins humming and vibrating, gaining volume with each passing second. As well as the noise, the door also begins forming a small circular hole directly in the center. As the noise grows louder, the hole becomes wider. The colors and shape of the gaping hole are practically identical to the one formed in the rock from before. Slowly but surely, the hole grows wide enough to engulf the entire door and leave behind nothing but a solid white shape. The shape glows brightly and creates a breeze flowing inward. It lifts the man's beard from his chest, and Rafa's shaggy fur can be seen blowing all over. The longer the white shape exists, the stronger the suctionlike breeze becomes, eventually to the point that the man must readjust his footing to brace himself.

Clutching his small dog, now with both arms, the man takes a step forward. The suction becomes much stronger, forcing the man to take another step and another. Within six or seven steps, the old man is face to face with the blinding light. One step more, and his foot travels directly through as if there was nothing even there. He braces his head down, holds Rafa tightly, and squints at the light. The noise is becoming too loud to bear, and the man is only left with a single option. With a final step, he enters the light and moves out of the vast, black emptiness.

His eyes are shut firmly, but his beard and Rafa's fur are no longer blowing about. His body is tensed and braced for some sort of impact, but nothing seems to be happening at all. Slowly and cautiously, he opens his eyes to a large, circular room. The ceiling is equally tall as the monolithic door was, and the ancient rock walls are covered in moss and vines. The man first looks back to see a small stone door directly behind him. The door is barely any bigger than the man; in fact, he may even have trouble fitting through it with his backpack on. Around the room, five other similar-sized doors can be seen. One is made of wood, another of ice. One appears to be made of grass, and the final two look to be made of mud and water. The man squints toward the one made of flowing water. There doesn't appear to be any natural water source nearby to create such a door.

He takes a step forward to the center of the room but quickly stops and tenses his shoulders again as the doors begin to hum. This time, the hum doesn't sound like a choir; each individual door has its own unique sound. The hum becomes softer and louder, as if trying to find harmony with one another. The man slightly relaxes his tension again and scans his surroundings once more. In the center of the room sits a hexagonal altar. It only comes up to about the old man's waist in height but is approximately one meter in width from corner to corner. In the middle of the altar rests the corpse of a Sugar Wing, a small, birdlike animal that very few have ever witnessed. Legend states that these animals sleep within clouds and only require the water from raindrops to survive. They can live up to eight hundred years, and some believe they are bearers of good fortune. It's said that if you hear a Sugar Wing singing, then you're blessed to be given a prosperous life and a painless death. The Sugar Wing has never been studied closely, because when they die, they fall from the sky like a blazing phoenix and no one can ever hunt down the remains.

High above the altar is a hole in the ceiling, very similar to the ones from the boulder and the eye-covered door. This one is only slightly different because it appears to be sheltered by a translucent film. Flying animals occasionally glide over it, but none appears to notice the gaping hole right beneath them. Directly centered within the hole is the Moon of Pyre, one of three moons that circles the planet, and quite easily the largest.

The old man looks back down to the room around him and does so in perfect timing. Just as he looks away from the sky, a blinding pillar much larger than all the previous comes pouring down from the moon. The old man covers his dog's eyes and closes his own to avoid losing his sight at the sheer brightness and color. The humming comes to a stop, and the blinding light begins to fade. As the old man reopens his eyes, he almost immediately holds his breath and becomes still. Standing around the room in front of each door is a colorful, glowing silhouette of many different shapes and sizes. Wasting no time, the glowing silhouettes walk forward to the altar. The shape of a tall, heavyset woman in front of the wooden door. A long-haired male who stands at half the height of the old man from the ice. Two almost identical thin figures, one from the grass door and one from the mud. A very large, muscular woman from the water door. And skipping gleefully past the old man, holding a small wooden toy, is the shape of a young child who came from the stone door.

The child turns back and playfully waves at the old man before meeting the others in the middle around the altar. The old man looks on, frozen and silent. Rafa wags his tail at the possibility of head scratches, but unfortunately for him, is held too tightly by his owner to escape. The six figures come together around the altar. They lock hands with one another and look down at the Sugar Wing in front of them, aside from the short male and child, who are almost at eye level with the deceased bird. Together they hum the tunes that each of the doorways had made just moments ago, occasionally changing pitch and volume until they reach a perfect harmony. The sound they create is sweet and warm. It feels comforting to listen to.

As the six varying figures continue to hum their tune, familiar strings of static form between them. It starts out as one or two occasional sparks but gradually transforms into an overwhelming wave of color atop the Sugar Wing. Before long, the once-dead animal between them begins to twitch and flutter. The ritual continues, and the Sugar Wing goes from lifeless to standing, standing to flying, and flying to singing. The whistle of the colorful animal is a perfect match to the hums of the six figures.

The Sugar Wing suddenly flies straight up as if it were going to leave, but stalls midair, perfectly centered in front of the glowing moon above. Like a fiery comet, the creature comes plummeting downward and charges directly through one of the six glowing silhouettes. The figure explodes into thousands of shimmering sparks, and the bird returns to the sky to repeat its process. One by one, the blazing animal shatters those standing around the altar until nothing is left of them but twinkling fragments. The pieces stay motionless in the air until the bird is finished with its task. It lands back on its stone resting place, and as if the entire cosmos came crashing inward, each kaleidoscopic particle furiously circles the altar in a beautiful display of color and motion.

Within the blink of an eye, the radiant shards enter the Sugar Wing's body, and a blinding flash of light consumes the entire room. The old man turns his back and shields his and his dog's eyes. As the light subsides, a choir of voices calls out to the man and his dog.

"Are you all right?" they ask.

The man struggles to respond. He stands still for a moment before turning back. "I-I am. Yes," he speaks out.

"Good." The voices ring throughout the chambers like a terrifyingly beautiful song. The man looks to the center of the room to no longer see a Sugar Wing or colorful figures standing within it. Instead, floating before him is a six-eyed, winged creature hovering just above the altar. A Fallen stares directly at the old man and Rafa. "Let's get you back where you belong then."

Chapter 9

The Right Path

What the old man and his dog just witnessed is legendary. The creation of an immortal being said to be ageless, nameless, and infinitely wise was just born into existence right before the two travelers' eyes. The creature floats gently above the stone altar, awaiting a response from the old man. Steadily, it goes about moving closer to the visitors within its temple.

"I can only return you to where you entered from. The large stone within Arboros swamp." The old man stares wide-eyed at the being in front of him. His mouth rests slightly open as if he were about to say something, but no words come out. "I can open the door now, and you should be on your—"

"Wait," the old man interjects. "I'm sorry to interrupt you, but if we're sent back to that swamp, we'll surely be killed." He looks down at his feet and then to his dog. Rafa wags his tail as if nothing unusual in the slightest is happening. He hangs from the man's arm with his tongue out and eyes partly closed, like he could fall asleep at any minute. "Back in the swamp, we were only a single day's travel from our goal. If I tell you our destination, would—"

"No," the Fallen interrupts. "Unfortunately, you should not have found your way to this shrine in the first place." The expressionless creature moves away from the stone door and floats peacefully across the large room to the water-based one instead. "You did, however, arrive here. That much can't be altered." The being pauses for a moment and then lets out a noise very similar to a sigh. "Here, this is as far as I can offer to take you." It reaches out a six-fingered hand to the liquid doorway. Each fingertip creates a subtle chime as it comes in contact with the water. Suddenly, as if a waterfall were to come crashing back upward, the dark-blue water flies in all directions to reveal a dim, dripping cave.

The old man looks to the Fallen and begins walking toward the freshly opened door. A staircase made of nothing but water leads upward to a partially lit night sky. The moon can be seen barely peeking through the top of the opening as the man tilts his head upward to get a clearer view.

"Your journey has put you through much trouble already. Consider this your good fortune for hearing a Sugar Wing's song," the Fallen jests to the old man as he continues looking up the stairway. The man smiles. He turns around, beginning to speak, but the room is now empty. Each of the previous doors has vanished, and nothing remains but the altar within the center. The old man laughs a short, nervous chuckle. He glances around once more before turning back to the door and warily stepping out onto the first liquid step. His foot lands firmly as if it were solid and carries no water as he lifts it away. He looks toward the top again. A hand reaches out to pet Rafa's head, ruffling his fur and scratching his ears. With no other place to go, the man walks up the staircase and back into the natural world.

Surrounding the two travelers, a variety of aquatic life can be seen swimming around the staircase. Plants rest deep on the ground below, and with each step, the two come closer to the exit. The fish pay no attention to the old man and his dog. Rafa even lets out a few playful barks as they pass by, but they act oblivious to the tourists within their domain.

The air feels cool; a gentle breeze rolls its way down the stairway. It blows the beard and shaggy fur of the two softly back and forth as they climb higher. The man looks back to the temple behind him to see nothing but dark, deep water. No doorway. Every step he takes, another stair behind him is engulfed by the dark-blue liquid. The man looks forward again to his final steps. As his head breaks the surface, the surroundings are familiar yet different. The occasional swampy trees and moss cover the riverbanks, but this is no longer the swamp. Bugs buzz about, but they are no longer mosquitos and gnats. The ever-nearing land is covered with flowers and short grass. Weeds interlace between the two, but this place is no life-threatening jungle.

This location has a calming atmosphere. Moonlight shines brightly to a dirt path within the trees, perpendicular to the old man and Rafa. The small dog furiously sniffs the air and kicks about within the old man's arms, wanting to be freed. The man tightens his dog's sky-blue bandanna and gently pats his head, assuring him that he can feel ground again soon. As the two take their last steps from the watery cave, the man places

his friend back onto safe, dry land. He looks back to watch the water flood its way down the remaining stairwell and cover it into nothingness.

Rafa is already relieving himself on a nearby tree, and the old man decides to join him. Once finished, the two immediately head off in the same direction. They walk with purpose and confidence in their steps. The old man looks to the treetops above while carefully avoiding loose rocks and roots below, all without ever glancing down. Rafa marks a few more locations along the beginning of the trail, weaving back and forth to each side. He smells the grass and even chews on a few tall blades of onion hair.

The man has yet to look down from the stars above him. His face doesn't smile, but neither does it frown. Emotionless and tired, the old man contentedly travels down the overgrown dirt path. It isn't long before the two travelers become three. A large, fat rodent scurries out of its hole from underneath a tree stump. It stops directly in the path of the old man and his dog. The chubby animal has one large eye directly in the middle of its head, as well as two more smaller eyes that rest on antennas to its side. The dark-orange-furred creature flaunts its stocky rump back and forth in front of Rafa as if it were completely unaware or teasing him. Two thin, short tails flop around behind the animal, leaving tiny marks in the dirt.

Indigenous to only a very small area just outside of Arboros, this creature is a buskerrat. The name probably sounds familiar because it's really just two common words mashed together, busker and rat. It got its name from the fact that it looks like a fat, little rodent and has curious tendencies to willingly approach almost any person for donations of food. They stand around, dancing and playing with their tails in hopes that they'll receive a tip in the form of bread or vegetables from the unsuspecting patrons. Some people consider them a nuisance, although most enjoy the animal's company and will gladly offer a morsel of food to the hardworking creature while on their picnics or walks.

Unluckily for it, Rafa sees it as neither a nuisance nor pleasant company. All the furry little dog recognizes is a potential game for him to chase around. So off he goes, not as quick as in the past, but on the hunt, regardless. The buskerrat zigs and zags away from its pursuer, although Rafa doesn't follow suit. He trails sluggishly behind, struggling to keep up as the game escapes him. Over a stone and across a puddle, the buskerrat shows no handicap for the old dog. Zigging, zagging, zipping around, but Rafa has barely kept his eyes on the fat, orange rodent. Up a stump and taking to the air, the buskerrat leaps powerfully forward, latching itself onto a nearby tree. Climbing high, away it goes, while Rafa still stands winded on the ground. The old dog pants heavily and flops to the dirt while his owner looks on with an endearing gaze.

Careful not to spook the tired dog, the man walks up from behind and lifts his friend from the trail and back into the safe comfort of his arms. Rafa groans at being lifted and closes his eyes as soon as he is securely held. The dog snorts and grunts with each of the old man's steps. Looking down at his fluffy pal, the man slows his pace, so as to not disturb the tired dog so much.

The moon is beginning to fall further away. The two travelers have been on this path for almost an hour. Trees that surround the trail have become fewer and farther between, but the ones that do reside in this part of the forest are thick and enormously tall. Even four of the old men would have difficulty wrapping their arms around the trunks. The branches start high and hold a mixture of green and brown leaves. As the wind pushes across the sky, it occasionally brings down a few of the massive leaves in front of or on top of the man and his dog.

Ahead in the distance, a clearing can be seen in the pathway. The dirt trail fades away into a field of grass and flowers. Sparse weeds interlock with this space as well, but they only accentuate its natural beauty and complement the openness of the area nicely. Just beyond the grass field, a tiny log cabin can be seen resting in front of a massive wall of trees. The river curves inward and creates a shallow stream just beside the house and yard.

As the two come closer, it becomes plain to see that although cozy, this cabin hasn't been used in quite some time. Spiderwebs fill every corner, and a layer of dust coats every tucked-away cranny so heavily that you can see it in the dark. The boards of the porch creak and groan as the old man steps on to them. Two windows rest on either side of the door, shut tightly and covered from the inside by curtains. The old man reaches his hand above the doorframe and pulls away a long, thin wire hiding atop it.

The old man walks to a nearby pillar and momentarily places his dog on the wooden porch to gain access to both of his hands. He slides the wire across his palm and fingertips, stopping just before the end. He grips tightly and creates a small ninety-degree bend in the wire, then looks above him to the top of the pillar. His arm reaches upward, sliding the wire around the secretive roof of the tall post, scratching and sliding it back and forth until suddenly, a small metal object

comes flying off to the side. The man laughs and leaves his wire hanging from the column. He walks to where the metal object has fallen and ungracefully crouches down to his knees. The old man moves clunkily with stiff limbs but finds his way to the ground nonetheless.

Upon reaching the floor, he begins sliding his hands across it and glancing around at the dark wooden porch. Before long, his eyesight locks on to something. The old man crawls forward, reaching his hand out and picking up a small silver key. He grips the key tightly and struggles to stand up. He reaches out to the railing for support and grunts and pops his way back to his feet.

Rafa is now awake and stands up equally slow as his old friend. He comes to the old man's side, tail still wagging, and awaits entry to the house. The man looks back at the river. Arboros's golden glow can barely be seen shining above the distant tree line. He looks back to the door and fumbles around until a loud click echoes throughout the porch. The door creaks open, dragging across the floorboards.

A dusty, sparsely decorated room awaits the two inside. Frilly curtains and colorful rugs line the walls and floor. A large bed sits in the middle of the room, covered by an elegant, simple blanket. Nails line the walls, but no pictures remain hanging. A dresser sits beside the door, holding a small wooden bowl that the man places his key into. A dark brick fireplace is built into the wall, and beside it a large metal chest. Rafa makes his way to the bed but can only whine from the footing. The man smiles and walks inside. He shuts the door behind him and lifts his tired dog onto the bed. Rafa walks a few circles before finding a comfortable spot for his slumber and quickly begins snoring away.

The man approaches the large metal chest and reaches inside to reveal a few stacks of firewood, as well as some matches. He gently lays his pack along the floor, rolling his shoulders around and groaning at the relief from the weight.

Although the old wood won't burn very hot, the night air is mostly comfortable, plus the bed is outfitted with a multitude of sheets and blankets. The man builds a fire until it's bright enough to see and digs a few lanterns out from behind the metal chest. He lights three and places them around the perimeter of the room. The shack is small and seemingly empty besides a few pieces of furniture. It's a single room with only one door and five windows, two on the back and front walls and one on the wall opposite to the fireplace.

With the cabin now properly lit, the dust and cobwebs are even more apparent. A once-vibrant rug sits faded across the floor, while sun-bleached curtains hang over the windows. The man strolls around the room, rubbing his hand across walls and tracking a line through the dust on each window. He stares out longingly toward the yard before reaching down to place his matches. The man opens a small drawer attached to the stand that holds his keys. Inside, he tosses the matches and shuts it back quickly. As the drawer shuts, a few items can be heard rolling against each other inside the miniature dresser.

The man pauses for a moment, then looks back. His hand reaches out slowly to the handle and pulls the drawer open completely. Pens and paper ruffle against each other, as do the matches. Beneath all of the loose items, however, is something made of glass. The man reaches out, careful as he lifts it from the resting place. A small picture frame, the only one he's found so far within the house. The picture is old and covered with dust, much like everything else. The old man wipes it away gently and stares wide-eyed at what he found—a young couple getting married. The man in the photograph is tall and charming. He appears a bit rough around the edges but carries a friendly smile. His eyes squint at the sunlight, and he wears a dark-blue suit. His hair is long, brown, and scruffy, and his face is rough like the rest of him. Tightly trimmed facial hair covers his mouth and cheeks. The bride, however, is undeniably stunning. She wears a short summer wedding dress, and her brown-and-blonde hair is curled ever so gently down her neck and ears, stopping just around her shoulders. Her eyes are warm and caring. Light brown like chocolate, staring wide into the camera. Her smile is infectious, and just looking at it makes the old man laugh to himself. Her beauty is overpowering to the rest of the picture. Everything else fades away when you stare at her. It's as if an angel came down from heaven to marry a goofy, scruffy man. They stand in front of a massive tree growing atop a hill. The tree is large, like the ones surrounding the trail, but this one sits completely alone in the field. Bright-pink leaves cling to its branches and rain down above the bride and groom.

The man clutches the picture tightly and carries it with him to the bed. He lays it on the pillow across him and unlaces his boots to lie down. The fire crackles throughout the night, only dying off around sunrise. The old man and Rafa sleep well into the afternoon, snoring and grumbling all night long. Over the course of the night, the sleepy dog finds his way up to his friend's chest and sleeps the rest of the night there. When the old man finally opens his eyes, he first looks to his dog, still in peaceful slumber. He lies still for a moment, turning to grasp the picture frame from last night. He stares on, studying every part of the image a hundred times over. Rafa has yet to wake

up, so the man pries himself away from the bed and gently pets his friend to alert him of the new day.

Rafa's eyes flutter awake, trying to fall back asleep. The man picks up his friend and sets him on the ground in an attempt to shake the sleepiness out of him. The old dog stands tiredly on the floor, his tail slowly wagging. The man laces up his boots and quickly snags the picture frame from the bed. He doesn't make his sheets or clean up the fireplace, just grabs his bag and prepares to leave. The key he leaves sitting on the stand as he opens the door. As he's exiting, something catches his eye from the drawer where he found the picture. His eyes glance back, and he reaches inside to find a small piece of paper. A picture with no frame. A tiny, tan-colored puppy sitting together with an old man and woman. They sit together in front of a funnel cake booth, the old man in the photo covered around his mouth and beard with powdered sugar. His hand is wrapped tightly with bandages, similar to the puppy's legs and stomach.

The old man laughs aloud and pretends to throw a couple of punches into the air before squeezing the paper tightly and placing it in his pocket. He looks back to his dog and whistles him over. Rafa meanders to the old man and exits the house first. The man bothers not with locking or even shutting the door. He leaves the place as if he never expects to return. His dog requires a bit of assistance down the stairs before the two begin another walk. The old man looks back at the cabin and river briefly before strolling around its side to a hidden path between the trees.

The two venture in, although on this trail, the man is the one taking the lead. He occasionally stops to look down at his dog. Rafa's tail is wagging, although his head hangs low. His posture is weak, and the dog occasionally trips or stumbles throughout the walk. The man keeps a close eye on his friend, a worried expression across his face. The two walk for almost an hour before the sounds of footsteps are reduced to only two. The old man pauses at the sound of a small thud, and his eyes grow wide. His brows rise, and he quickly jerks around to see the small, sweet Rafa lying motionless on his side. Breathing slowly in and out, the old dog looks to the man, who is already running in his direction. The man wastes no time falling to his knees and hurriedly but carefully scoops the small dog off of the ground and into his lap.

Chapter 10

The End

The contents of his bag lay scattered throughout the dirt. Herbs, liquids, mushrooms, bandages. Rafa is lying still within the old man's lap as he mixes together a concoction of assorted ingredients. He tries desperately to feed his old friend, but all the dog can do is breathe. Even now, the tail of the dog is gently wagging across his friend's leg. The scraggly mutt inhales and exhales slowly, his fur barely rising and falling with each breath.

The afternoon sun is bright, even through the tree line. Slivers of light pour down from above into the dog's gentle brown eyes. The man turns his position to offer his companion shade. Birds are loud today, but their songs feel quiet and distant. The breeze, tree branches, grass, animals, and even distant water all come together to create an orchestra of natural music.

A variety of winged insects fly above the old man and his dog, buzzing and whirring by their heads, swarming together to create the sole dark clouds within the sky. The larger ones feed off of the smaller, and even the largest are consumed by birds larger than them. Countless lives snuffed out every second. What makes the life of an insect any less valuable than that of something larger? Bugs are not mourned like people. Nor are birds, frogs, or squirrels. Is it the intelligence of the life form that makes it worth mourning? The lifespan, the emotional connection to another, or its impact on the world around it? A life is still a life. Perhaps each life matters to at least one other, if nothing else.

The sunlight pours carefully throughout the canopy of branches above, perfectly making its way through any available openings and scattering across the dirt trail below. Light travels an unfathomable distance just to disappear into dusty, old pathways. A warm breeze swoops in from the east, shaking old leaves from high above limbs. They sway down gracefully, twirling across the empty space of warm summer air. Nothing can be done to stop a leaf from falling. You can hold the leaf with your own hand, but eventually you too would collapse. The leaf can be protected and nurtured from the harsh environment, but even the tree itself will one day die. An old tree losing many leaves over its lifetime is only natural. One day, if the tree survives without being cut, it will be left with no leaves at all. Too old to grow more, yet still just too young to die. It spends its last season sparse and empty. Holding desperately on to each final leaf before it no longer has the strength to carry any more.

The old man has yet to remove his gaze from the dog, locked directly onto the barely moving Rafa. His hands fly around, grabbing herb after herb, tool after tool, attempt after attempt. He grits his teeth. His eyes clench tightly, like his fist, and his brow furrows deeply. He takes in a deep breath and lets go of the tension in his face, continuing to mix together herbal remedies. The few that the old dog manages to keep down don't appear to have any effect.

"I'm so sorry, buddy."

The only words that the old man is able to choke out. His hands move slower and slower as time passes. The determination in the old man's eyes glazes over into tears and frustration. He looks into Rafa's face. The fur around his mouth is grayer than it is black. His eyes squint when they manage to stay open, and his dark-brown eyes only look toward the old man. The hair covering his small body is matted and tangled from such a long journey. Even his tiny black nose is becoming dry from lack of saliva. The old dog has droopy ears that hang slightly past his head. They lay motionless against his face, being scratched and brushed softly by his partner.

Rafa struggles to lean upward toward the old man and partially opens his mouth. Lifting the animal from his lap, he brings his dog close to his face and falls back against the tree behind him. The man closes his eyes tightly and scrunches his face in sadness. A warm, soft tongue barely caresses the old man's cheek, just enough to wipe away a tear. He holds his friend close, the old man shaking and trembling.

Sunlight is traveling across the ground as the two sit together. The old man attempts to stand, although he never removes his arms from Rafa. Struggling to find his balance, the old man sways and topples away from the tree until finally finding his footing in a kneeling position. He rises sluggishly, wincing at each echoing pop throughout his joints. Once on

his feet again, the man uses his right hand to reach down and retrieve his bag. He bothers not with attaching it securely, instead tossing it over a single shoulder and leaving its contents scattered across the ground.

His feet drag their bodies away from the path, heading between the towering trees and off into the wilderness. Grass and weeds become taller as the two journey farther in. The fragile stems sweep against the old man's thighs, concealing the ground below. Running water grows louder as the man and Rafa approach a rocky slope. The decline is gentle, covered with smooth, wet stones and sand. Air becomes cooler as the two approach, while the sun shines brighter with no more trees to block it.

The water is crystal clear, barely knee deep in the centermost location. Fish swim upstream over more flat, smooth stones resting below them. Their colors reflect vibrantly off of the light. Red, purple, pink, green. Every fish has its own distinct size and color. They scatter away as the old man steps directly into the running water and wades out deeper. He comes to a stop nearly a quarter of the way in and gently leans forward toward the cool, refreshing liquid. With a cupped hand, he brings his dog a small drink. He holds it near Rafa's mouth, but the dog has no energy to consume it.

Streams of water quickly drain from between the old man's fingers. He reaches back down and tries again with a fresh hand, but the result is the same. The old man repeats this process over and over. Nearly an hour passes of him trying to offer his tired dog a drink, but no result comes from the labor. He travels back to the riverbank to sit among the rocks and sand, boot-covered feet still in the water as he rests. A hand reaches for the water again, but this time he only wets the fingertips. He brings the hand back to his dog and slowly works it throughout the tangled fur. He's cautious to not pull and carefully removes the tangles from his old friend.

The two sit together on the bank as day becomes dusk. They watch the fish, listening to the river flow downstream. The old man pets his dog, offering the infrequent words he can muster.

"Good boy," he whispers. "You're a good boy, Rafa."

The old dog looks up at the old man after hearing his name. The two lock eyes, and the man gently tightens his embrace. Rafa acts calm and quiet. He doesn't whimper or groan. All he's been able to do since collapsing is breathe. Slowly but inevitably, the breaths begin to halt. Rafa blinks less frequently, not removing his vision from the man.

"Thank you for being my best friend. I love you, buddy."

The slightest movement from Rafa's tiny paw nudges the old man's arm. All the man can do now is smile for his friend. Throughout the tears and sniffles, the man keeps his eyes wide and continues to smile.

"Tell her I said hello. I'll find you both soon enough."

His body is no longer supporting its own weight. His head goes limp against the old man's arms as his lungs refuse to expand. Rafa's eyes no longer blink. They lie open and empty, staring blankly into the old man. The light within them is hazy, glazed over. The shadows of the two travelers expand into darkness. Night has fallen over the weeping man.

The old man places his bag back onto both shoulders and comes to a stand once more. As he travels back where they sat

underneath the canopy of trees, the music of the forest plays a symphony of grief for the lonely traveler. He carries his small companion back onto the dirt path and onward to their destination. Nocturnal birds whistle a melancholic tune, the trees stand still and silent as the man walks between them.

Ahead in the distance, a clearing begins to form out of the darkness. Moonlight shines down brightly into a large, empty field. It creeps through the exit of the wooded trail like honey flowing across a table. The brown dirt trail suddenly ends and becomes a sheet of vibrantly green grass. The field is circular and enveloped by a wall of trees. In the center, the grass slopes upward, forming a tall hill.

Atop the hill sits a familiar sight. The man walks expressionlessly forward, no smile to have reached his destination, a gigantic tree covered in thousands of pink flowers and leaves. The bark is a dark, rich brown. It travels high and wide, yet grows perfectly hidden in this secret field surrounded by woods. As the man nears the field, a small blue light shines beside his head, quickly flickering brightly and then disappearing into the night.

His wet boots carry mud into the soft, short grass. Each step leaves an impression behind him, clearly visible by the full moon. It hovers high above the night sky, partially to the left of the large, colorful tree. Stars fill the emptiness around it, twinkling and shining alongside. The man looks up to the tree from the base of the hill, pausing for a moment before returning his vision to the ground and walking upward. His hands are full with the small, shaggy dog. He carries him softly and gingerly, taking his time with each step up the hill.

As he walks, the straps of his bag flop against his shoulders. Having now been mostly emptied, the large khaki travel sack rests lightly upon his back. His watch catches the reflection of the moon and shines it back away from the man's arm. It no longer ticks or tells the time. Stuck at nine forty-seven, it's no more than a decoration at this point. The man lifts his head, taking his eyes away from the ground to instead look briefly at the tree. His eyes are still wet and red, but his face shows no emotion. The arms of the old man continue to tremble, his fingers clutch into Rafa's fur as he nears the top.

The world around him is calm, peaceful. Here stands a tall, weathered old man, outfitted in travel gear, carrying a large bag that doesn't weigh much, but more than most humans his age could manage. He stands in front of the breathtakingly gorgeous tree on a cool, clear night, completely alone, holding the body of his closest and only friend. He's not a grand adventurer or a terribly important person in the overall scheme of the world. He's only an old man. An old man who walked from his house to this tree. Now that he stands at his goal, he carefully drops the bag from his shoulders that he spent so much effort to bring with him.

The man softly places his luggage on the ground underneath the large tree and starts the process of kneeling down himself. He places his dog onto the ground beside his bag and begins pulling away at the grass in front of him. With his bare hands he digs and claws his way through the cold, brown dirt. His fingernails are dirty, and his hands are scratched. The skin across his knuckles is dry, cracking away from his body while he digs.

More turquoise lights appear and disappear around the oblivious old man. He turns over the ground, one scrape at a time, until a shallow hole is formed in front of him. The old man looks to his friend, who lies motionless on the bed of grass. His arms reach out slowly, lifting and moving the dog into the hole he has just dug. His hands offer a last touch to the dog's fur; leaning down, he kisses his friend and whispers a farewell into Rafa's ear. The man struggles to breathe as he begins to cry at the loss of his companion. Tears stream down his cheeks. He fills the hole, handful by handful, until the small, tan-colored dog is nothing but a memory.

His dirt-covered hands make their way to the large khaki bag, and he opens the top flap. Not much remains inside his carrying case except the small jar of glowing flowers from Arboros and a square black package, previously covered in the blue cloth that was gifted to Rafa. The old man shakes the jar of flowers to create a sparkling dust of color before opening it and removing one from the container. He places the green flower onto the grave and watches momentarily as the ember, like pollen, floats away into the air. The remaining flowers he keeps inside the jar, which he sits directly against the tree.

His wrinkled hands shake as he reaches forward to the black package. He opens it with his eyes shut tightly, tearing away the tape and weeping with his head tilted downwards. Removing the lid, a small ceramic jar can be seen sitting inside. It has no intricate art or decorations covering the sides or lid. A simple yellow urn. Nothing more.

The old man opens his eyes briefly to gaze into the precious cargo that he delivered so carefully. Air begins to swirl around him as the night breeze rolls in from over the treetops. Hundreds, possibly thousands of turquoise fireflies take to the air around the old man and throughout the moonlit field. Carefully, he opens the urn and closes his eyes once more as the ashes pour from its side. Pink flowers fall around the fireflies while the wind lifts the dark ash into the sky. The man leans back on his knees and stares longingly into the tree. His vision watches the stars, the moon, the lights. He watches as the ashes are taken away from him, and he is left with nothing but the world around.

He cries, gripping the empty urn. The turquoise lights continue to flicker while the breeze dies back down into stillness. There the old man sits, having finished his travels. Left alone in a vast world, he has nothing left to accomplish. The old man stays resting on his tired, weary knees, eyes peering upward through an ocean of tears.

His journey is finally complete.

"To my little buddy Rafa. Thank you for all the adventures we shared, I look forward to seeing you again one day. You're a good boy."

DC Smith

is an author and voice actor based out of Northern Georgia. *The Tree With Pink Leaves* is his first published work and is inspired by the many years of adventures spent with his dog Rafa. Having always lived with a deep passion for the art of storytelling, he began writing in grade 2 and has since been determined to entertain every person he has met thereafter.

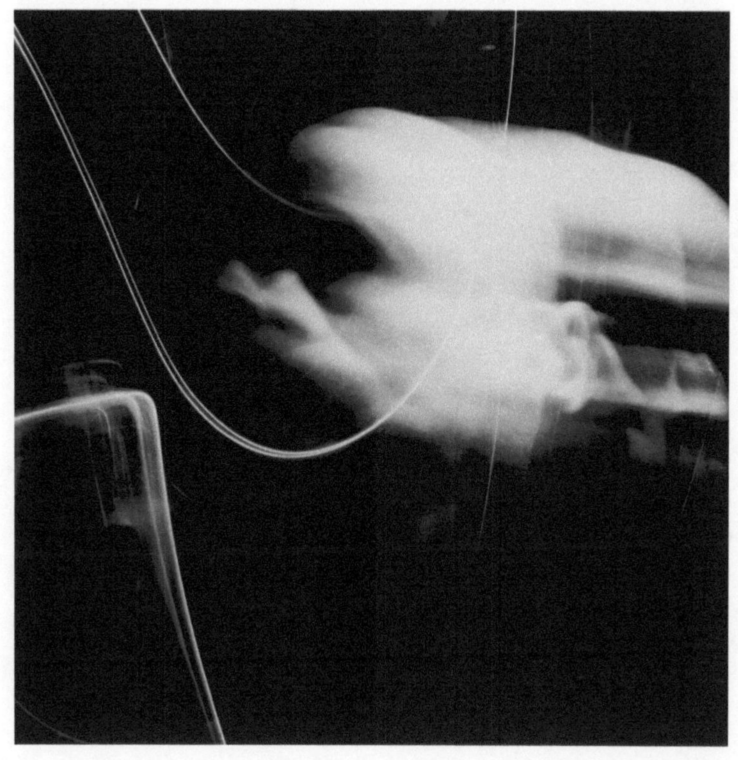

Deiniol Owen

Based in England, UK, Deiniol Owen is the Illustrator behind Fulmar Illustration. A strong interest in birds and nature led him to study environmental conservation, but due to a lifelong passion for art, he decided on pursuing that path instead. Deiniol's hand drawn illustrations are produced using the traditional method of a dipping pen and ink, this allows him to create organic lines and textures as opposed to the refined lines of a modern pen.

www.ingramcontent.com/pod-product-compliance
Lightning Source LLC
Chambersburg PA
CBHW060802310726
48980CB00002B/199
* 9 7 8 0 5 7 8 8 7 2 1 7 9 *